A LITTLE BIT LOUDER AND A WHOLE LOT WORSE

2019

A LITTLE BIT LOUDER AND
A WHOLE LOT WORSE

JAMES SCHLARMANN

First published in print in 2020 by Blue Lens

Blue Lens is an imprint of Blue Lens Films Limited
71-75 Shelton Street, Covent Garden, London, WC2H 9JQ, UK

Text Copyright © James Schlarmann 2019
Cover Design © Blue Lens Films 2020
Cover Art by Irving Martinez

The moral right of the author to be identified as the creator of this work
has been asserted by the Copyright, Design and Parents Act 1988

All rights reserved
This book is sold subject to the condition that it shall not, by
way of trade or otherwise, be lent, resold, hired, copied or
otherwise circulated in any form of binding or cover, in part
or entirety, without the prior written permission of the publisher.

The works contained within this book are satirical fiction.
Any resemblance to actual events does not represent a true and accurate
account of the facts. The views expressed within this are satirical and
may not represent the views of the author or the publisher.

A CIP Catalogue record for this book is available from the British Library

ISBN 978-1-913408-10-7

3 5 7 9 10 8 6 4 2

Printer and binder may vary between territories of production and sale

The environmental impact of producing this book and distributing it to the reader has
been fully offset by the publisher as part of their commitment to net carbon neutrality

The contents of this book first appeared on the satirical websites *The Political Garbage Chute, Alternative Facts, The Pastiche Post, Satirical Facts, Alternative Science,* and *Not Really News*

To read more satirical news stories from James Schlarmann, visit:

politicalgarbagechute.com
alternativelyfacts.com
pastichepost.com
satiricalfacts.com
alternative-science.com
notreally.news

Also by James Schlarmann
2015: The Best of The Worst of Times
2016: Well, That Happened
2017: The Year That Was (But Shouldn't Have Been)
2018: None of This is Normal
2015-2018: Reality for Satirical Times

Other Satire from Blue Lens

Devin Nunes Had a Meeting (Allegedly) by Ben Fletcher
Devin Nunes Had a Farm by Ben Fletcher
FIGGERED: My Dad is Bigger Than Your Dad (Donald Trump Jr) by Ben Fletcher
FIGURING: My Don Jr. Picture Book (Eric Trump) by Ben Fletcher
Not Much Happened (Anthony Scaramucci) by Ben Fletcher

CONTENTS

JANUARY 2019

Trump Boys "Playing Government" With Daddy During Shutdown	3
Obama Offers to Fill-In as President During Government Shutdown	5
Prime-Time Trump Border Address Will Be Broadcast in English, Spanish, and Moron	7
Mexico Agrees to Pay for Commercial Time During Trump's Border Wall Address	9
Asshole Itching to Give All His Asshole Opinions	11
Trump Asks Legal Team If Sitting Presidents Can Be Indicted or Impeached During Shutdown	13
Trump: Telling Sarah Huckabee Sanders Not to Give Briefings 'Only Way to Keep Her From Lying'	16
God Denies Any Collusion With Trump Campaign	18

FEBRUARY 2019

A LITTLE BIT LOUDER AND A WHOLE LOT WORSE

President's Plane Renamed "Air Force Individual-1"	23
Trump Tells Secret Service to Investigate Pelosi's 'Threatening Sarcastic Clapping'	25
Trump: It's 'Treasonous' That Andrew McCabe and Others Put Country Ahead of Loyalty to Him	28
Mexico Agrees to Pay for National Emergency as Long as Trump Can Prove It Exists	31
Kellyanne Conway: National Emergency at Border 'Much Bigger and Worser Crisis' Than Bowling Green Massacre	33
Courier Hands Cohen Check Signed by President Trump Just Before Entering Capitol Building	36
Jim Jordan Shreds Cohen Testimony: 'Total Waste of Taxpayer Dollars' That 'Didn't Get Into Benghazi Even Once'	39

MARCH 2019

Trump: 'I Didn't Obstruct Justice, I Just Tried to Impede an Investigation!'	45
Trump Regrets Lying About Lying About Telling Michael Cohen to Lie About Him Lying	47
Trump Asked Woman If the Bible He Signed is 'Any Good or Not'	50

CONTENTS

J.K. Rowling Says You Didn't Actually Read Harry Potter Novels	54
White Nationalism Ban Briefly Brings Down President's Facebook Page	56

APRIL 2019

Barr Investigating If Obama Administration Forced Trump to Be Lifelong Lying Conman and Racist Idiot	61
Barr Exonerates Dozens of Criminals Who Were Arrested After Scooby-Doo's Investigations	64
Trump Shouts 'NO COLLUSION, NO OBSTRUCTION!' in Every Child's Face at White House Egg Roll	67
Doctors Rushing to Perform Spinal Implants on Congressional Democrats Still on the Fence About Impeaching Trump	70
Pelosi Wishes 'the Founders Had Given Us Some Tool by Which to Hold a President Accountable'	73
Trump to Give Robert E. Lee Posthumous Medal of Freedom	75

MAY 2019

Trump: "Bob Mueller Shouldn't Testify Because He'd Exonerate Me Way Too Much!"	81

A LITTLE BIT LOUDER AND A WHOLE LOT WORSE

Trump Promises: "We're Only Covering-Up How Innocent I Really, Truly Am, I Pinky Swear!"	84
Gym Jordan: "Sure Trump Broke the Law, but What Right Do the American People Have to Know the Details?"	87
Hillary to Trump Jr.: "Oh, You Already Testified Before Congress? I Can Benghazi How Difficult That Might Be"	90
Mitch McConnell: "Trump's Not Above the Law, It Just Doesn't Apply to Him"	93
Donald Trump Jr.'s Book on Hold While Doctors Fish the Crayon out of His Nose	96

JUNE 2019

After 14 Hours in the UK Without Fox News, President Convinced Donald Trump Is Danger to America	101
Steven Crowder Hates Socialism so Much He Thinks Trump Should Nationalize YouTube and Force Them to Monetize Him	104
Trump Economic Adviser: Eliminating Minimum Wage Will Result in 0% Unemployment	107
Texas Business Has Been Making Millions on Its "Lunch With Ted Cruz" Escape Room	110
Local Conservative Outraged at Liberal's 'Vulgar Display of Empathy and Compassion'	113

CONTENTS

DNC Informs Registered Dems Who They Should Think Won First Debates	116

JULY 2019

Fox News Offers Time Slot Before Tucker Carlson to Kim Jong-Un	121
Trump Blames 4th of July Rain on 'Bob Mueller's Team of Angry Democrats'	124
Fox News Hires David Dennison as New Programming Director	127
British Ambassador Promises to Stop Having Opinions That Are Based in Fact	130
Trump Warns His Enemies Not to Interfere in 2020 Election by Voting for the Democrats	133
NRA Backs Law Allowing Gun Sales After Shop Is Closed	136
Eric Trump: 95% of Unicorn Breeders Support His Father	139
Trump Campaign Manager Promises His Boss Will 'Keep America on the White Track'	141

AUGUST 2019

A LITTLE BIT LOUDER AND A WHOLE LOT WORSE

Lahren: "Mermaids Are White, Just Like Santa and Jesus!"	145
Tucker Carlson: "It's Not Racist If I Call Them the N-Word in My Head"	148
Evangelical Libertarian: "Jesus Died on the Cross to End Progressive Taxation"	150
Scientists Can Finally Prove Which Trump Can Outsmart a Bag of Hammers	153
Trump Calls Domino's Pizza "the Enemy of the People" for Forgetting His Hot Wing Dipping Sauce	156
Man Chanting 'Send Her Back' Can't Locate His Home State on a Map	160
Mexican Government Releases Detailed Audit of How Much They've Paid for Trump's Wall so Far	164

SEPTEMBER 2019

Trump Hereby Orders Every State to Change Its Name to "Alabama"	169
NRA Supports Universal Background Checks and Waiting Periods for Vaping Products	171
Fearing Another Whistleblower, President Bans Tea Kettles From White House	174

CONTENTS

John Adams Once Called the King of England for Dirt on Thomas Jefferson	177
Gingrich Explains Subtle Differences Between Consensual Blowjobs and Coercing Foreign Governments to Investigate Political Rivals	180

OCTOBER 2019

Jim Jordan: "We Can't Impeach Trump Before Impeaching Joe Biden"	185
Trump Checks Democratic Primary Polls to Figure out Who Foreign Countries Should Investigate for Corruption Next	188
Donald Trump Jr. Enrolls at Electoral College to 'Learn to Become an Electrician'	192
President Says Constitution Signers Were 'Never Trumpers' Who Planned a Coup Against Him	195
Eric and Donald Trump Jr. Are Going to Scare White House Trick-Or-Treaters as 'Pointy-Headed Ghosts'	199

NOVEMBER 2019

New York City Real Estate Values Have Tripled Since Trump Announced He Left	203
Trump Wants Purple Heart for Getting Ego Bruised by Impeachment	207

Hillary Clinton Offers to Represent President Trump in His Impeachment Trial	210
President Requires Dirt on Joe Biden Before Pardoning Any Turkeys	214
Devin Nunes: "It's Time to Impeach the Media"	217

DECEMBER 2019

Study Shows 100% of Abortions You Don't Get Still None of Your Business	223
Trump Demands House Vote on His Articles of Impeachment Using 'Electoral College Rules'	226
White House: Articles of Impeachment Don't Have Enough Pictures so Trump Can't Understand Them	230
McConnell Promises to Hold Impeachment Trial in Moscow	233

JANUARY

JANUARY 2, 2019

Trump Boys "Playing Government" With Daddy During Shutdown

WASHINGTON, D.C. — President Donald Trump is presiding over yet another shutdown of the federal government under his watch. Now, over ten days after the fight over funding for his border wall met an impasse that caused the government to shutter itself until an agreement can be reached between Trump, the Democrats who now control the House, and Republicans in the Senate, word is that Donald Trump Jr. and his brother Eric have been dressing up as various government officials and mock-running the government with their father over the holiday break.

"A couple of days ago, Junior and Eric showed up dressed as Ben Carson and Wilbur Ross," one White House aide told us. "The president was really impressed with Junior's blackface. And said he looked just as urban as Secretary Carson."

Sources say that the trio of Trumps have been running around the White House, pretending to make big policy decisions and implement them, holding faux-cabinet meetings, and even holding an imaginary meeting in the Situation Room, where they pretended to watch President Trump order a nuclear strike on California for "being petulant libtards."

A LITTLE BIT LOUDER AND A WHOLE LOT WORSE

"The three of them were quite pleased with themselves," our source told us. "They were really laughing it up and having a great time. Eric even pretended to be the Attorney General and fired Robert Mueller, or who Eric called 'that mean man with all the facts about our criminal enterprise.' Same diff, really."

Reportedly, the president is considering leaving the government shut down so that his new, totally imaginary one can continue in its place. Our source within the White House says that several staffers are totally okay with that idea.

"Let's face it, Trump's no more the real president than Dubya was anyway," our source said. "The difference is that Bush was having strings pulled from the Vice-President's office, and Trump's getting his pulled from the Kremlin, like with the decision to pull out of Syria. Since most of Trump's accomplishments have been a figment of his imagination, he figured the whole government should be too."

The White House did not comment on this story.

JANUARY 7, 2019

Obama Offers to Fill-In as President During Government Shutdown

WASHINGTON, D.C. — Citing the fact that he already lives in Washington and is "kinda familiar" with the job duties, former President Barack Hussein Obama (D-Kenya) has offered to fill-in for President Trump, should the federal government remain shut down.

Obama, on his way out to pick up the dry cleaning for former First Lady Michelle Obama, was stopped by reporters and asked about the current government shutdown. For more than two weeks, President Donald Trump has been locked in a budgetary battle, demanding that Congressional Democrats agree to another $5 billion in funding for the southern border wall he promised to his base during the 2016 presidential election.

Obama said it would be a "shame if Republicans can't manage things even when they control literally almost the entire government." But that should a shutdown come to pass, he would step in for Trump.

"Hey, I've really enjoyed my time off after eight long years of actually working and not just tweeting and golfing," Obama said. "But if you guys need a pinch-president, I'll be your Huckleberry for a couple weeks… months…until Bob Mueller finishes his investigation — you know, whenever."

Obama said that while it may be "like riding a bike at first," he's sure he can "get back into the swing of things" in a relatively short period.

"Kinda feels like I still got my hands on the economy anyway," Obama said.

Constitutionally, Obama says he's on solid footing, as he'd only be serving using his "temporary Sharia president guidelines" which he secretly slipped into the Constitution in 2011, "just in case," he said.

"Besides, no one elected me to a third term; I'd just be sort of, you know, keeping the lights on and the seat warm," Obama said with a smile.

Security shouldn't be an issue, at least according to President Obama.

"I hid a key under a bush on the front lawn, so unless someone picked it up, I can let myself in," the former president said.

The White House did not respond to requests for comment on this story.

JANUARY 7, 2019

Prime-Time Trump Border Address Will Be Broadcast in English, Spanish, and Moron

WASHINGTON, D.C. — When President Trump delivers his prime time Oval Address on what he's calling a "crisis" at the southern border, his speech will be broadcast in English, Spanish, and the language of morons.

"Primarily the speech will be delivered in Trump's native tongue, but we knew that we'd need to get translations into English and Spanish on the fly," White House media communications liaison Tom Thompaulsen told reporters on the White House lawn today. "Finding someone to translate the president into English was pretty easy, but Stephen Miller purged the executive branch of anyone with even a vaguely Mexican-ish sounding name last year, so that was the tricky part."

Sources say that Trump's speech will be kept very brief — to about seven or eight minutes.

"He begged us to extend it so he could treat it like one of his campaign rallies during the mid-terms," Thompaulsen said. "That plan was a non-starter though because there was no way we could get enough books for a bonfire on such short notice. We were able to

A LITTLE BIT LOUDER AND A WHOLE LOT WORSE

convince him to keep his speech brief by reminding him he'd be in bed with the First Lady sooner if he kept it short. Once he confirmed Ivanka was in town this week, it was an easy sell, really."

The need for a translator at all was first vexing to the president, Thompaulsen revealed.

"We told him that the people who will understand his speech in moron aren't the ones who need to hear it," Thompaulsen said. "Those people hear people speaking moron in their ears from their morning commute with Hannity, to their evening hate-rage-jerk-off fest with Laura Ingraham and Hannity again later that night on Fox. It's the libtards that need to understand him, and libtards speak that hoity-toity form of language called 'English,' so here we are. Face to face. A couple of silver spoons."

With the government set to enter its third week in a shutdown stalemate, it's unclear just how much impact this Oval Office address will have. Thompaulsen says that Trump is committed to keeping the government closed for a very long time if he needs to secure border wall funding. There's another reason that Trump is confident that keeping the federal government closed is a good thing for him, in the end.

"His boss is totally okay with the United States government being shuttered," Thompaulsen said. "So, when your employer sends you a Kushner back-channel message to 'Keep it up, comrade,' you listen to that message."

This is a developing story.

JANUARY 8, 2019

Mexico Agrees to Pay for Commercial Time During Trump's Border Wall Address

MEXICO CITY, MEXICO — Mexican President Andrés Manuel López Obrador announced today that his country would pay for commercial time during an address from the Oval Office tonight, delivered by U.S. President Donald Trump.

Mr. Trump is expected to deliver a seven to eight minute address on what he is calling an ongoing "crisis" at the southern border between the U.S. and Mexico. The United States government is currently in a shutdown state because Trump has reached an impasse with a newly minted Democratic majority in the House over funding for the wall he wants to be built on the border. During the 2016 campaign, Trump promised the country over and over that Mexico would, in fact, be paying for the wall, but both the previous and the current Mexican president have flatly denied that chance.

"While the Mexican government stays steadfastly opposed to spending one dime of our taxpayers' money on this stupid wall," Obrador announced, "we have decided it's in the best interest of all North Americans if we buy commercial time to make sure truth and reality get equal time to delusion, racism, and Xenophobia."

A LITTLE BIT LOUDER AND A WHOLE LOT WORSE

President Obrador says he hopes that the commercial his government puts together will run in the middle of Trump's speech, but he realizes it will be so short, the networks might have to air the ad before or after the address.

"That's why we're going to buy enough time for two ads, one to air before, and one after," President Obrador explained. "Basically the first ad will be a voice-over Trump's face that says, 'Everything you're about to hear is total bullshit.' The commercial after the speech will be the same voice over the same picture of Donald, but this time it'll say, 'Everything you just heard was total bullshit.' We think it's a very effective message."

The White House did not comment on this story, as President Trump and White House Policy Adviser Stephen Miller were too busy crafting the right racist joke to open the Oval Office address.

JANUARY 12, 2019

Asshole Itching to Give All His Asshole Opinions

THE SHITE VALLEY, CALIFORNIA — From within his gated community, sitting in the living room of his 3200 square foot house overlooking the Pacific Ocean, Jim Jasper sits, patiently waiting for you to pay attention to him. Jim is an asshole with a bunch of opinions, and he's dying to give every single one of them to you, right now.

"I've spent a lifetime building up thoughts and feelings about a whole array of topics, and most of them are utterly atrocious," Jasper told us in a Skype interview. "You should hear my thoughts on the *Star Wars* prequels. Spoiler Alert: BEST FILMS NOT JUST IN FRANCHISE, BUT IN CINEMATIC HISTORY!"

And it's not just horrible, asshole opinions on movies that Jasper has. He'd like to share all kinds of opinions he has with you that he feels are "just as much stupid as they are nonsensical, or even flat out based on fiction."

"Honestly, I don't know why everyone thinks grilled cheese sandwiches are good," Jim says. "They're just melted cheese between two slices of bread. So what? You know what's really tasty? Canned sausages and a Diet Pibb. Fuck literally everything else."

A LITTLE BIT LOUDER AND A WHOLE LOT WORSE

Even on subjects, he admits he has no expertise, experience, or real interest in are not safe from Jim's opinions. In fact, he says, he might actually be more adamant and more emotionally invested in telling you those opinions than the ones on subjects he actually knows about, like rowboat design and manufacturing.

"Sure, I've been one of the world's most well-known and famous rowboat engineers for thirty years," Jim says. "But I have a real burning desire to sit you down, look you right in the eye, and tell you why I think New Kids on the Block surpassed the Beatles in terms of musicianship and songwriting, and more importantly, why you're an asshole if you don't agree with me."

That, Jim said, is the "real point in all this."

"It's not so much my opinion that white socks and sandals are the ONLY choices to make for footwear during the summer that excites me," Jim said. "It's the idea of getting to stab my finger into your chest and call you an asshole when you disagree with me. That's the real point in all of this."

Jasper will be touring the country this summer in a Winnebago with a P.A. speaker attached to it. He'll be screaming his opinions through the speaker starting at sunrise and concluding at sunset. Jim hopes to visit as many states as he can during his tour.

Early reviews of Jim's tour are mixed but made up of only very strong opinions.

JANUARY 14, 2019

Trump Asks Legal Team If Sitting Presidents Can Be Indicted or Impeached During Shutdown

WASHINGTON, D.C. — President Donald Trump has directed his sizable legal team to research and determine if a sitting president can be either indicted or impeached during a shutdown of the federal government.

"The president is simply wondering if he's actually the president of anything during a government shutdown," White House Deputy Jr. Media Secretary Tom Thompaulsen told reporters in the White House this morning. "No one should, like, read anything into this, okay? We're just asking for...a friend...who has orange skin. And probably committed crimes ranging from tax fraud to treason and may be indicted or impeached for them."

Thompaulsen paused, realizing what he'd just said.

"But again, to reiterate, the president is simply asking routine, hypothetical questions that every president asks when they've spent literally every moment of their presidency under federal investigation," Thompaulsen said. "This is just all so very blase, isn't it? What president that was helped into the Oval Office by a hostile foreign government wasn't also under heavy scrutiny and suspicion for being an

A LITTLE BIT LOUDER AND A WHOLE LOT WORSE

agent of that very same government? Ho-hum, fam. Ho-hum."

The federal government has entered its fourth week of being in a state of partial shutdown. This is now the longest-running such shutdown. Last year, Trump also oversaw a government shutdown around the same time. Despite telling both House Speaker Nancy Pelosi and Senate Minority Leader Chuck Schumer that he would "gladly" take the blame for this shutdown before it started, over the last four weeks, Trump has become increasingly more combative with the Democrats and has begun simply pegging the entirety of the blame on them.

Recent polling, however, shows that Trump is taking the overwhelming majority of the blame for his refusal to budge on over $5 billion in additional funding for a southern border wall. Trump ran his 2016 campaign largely on a promise to build a wall and force Mexico to pay for it. However, despite saying that a newly renegotiated trade deal with Mexico would offset the costs, the way trade deals actually work for people not buried inside Larry Laffer's cornhole means that argument really doesn't make much logical sense. Thompaulsen says the "fake news" is "too obsessed" with who cut the physical check for the wall.

"Look, does it really matter if Mexico pays for it, or if we pay for it? The point is someone will pay for it," Thompaulsen said, "and besides, if we just write 'From Mexico' on our tax payment checks, then pretty much that is like Mexico paying for it, right? Right? RIGHT?!"

President Trump was stopped on his way back into the White

JANUARY

House after his doughnuts and fried chicken run. Reporters asked him how long the shutdown will last.

"Well, that all depends. It depends on the Democrats," Trump shouted at the reporters. "And of course I mean the 14.5 trillion Angry Democrats on Bob Mueller's investigation. If they can't indict me, and if Congress can't impeach me during the shutdown, that would make this shutdown last bigly indefinitely, fam."

Donald Trump was elected to the presidency and lost the popular vote by historic margins. His approval ratings have never gone above 50% a single time during his tenure.

JANUARY 23, 2019

Trump: Telling Sarah Huckabee Sanders Not to Give Briefings 'Only Way to Keep Her From Lying'

WASHINGTON, D.C. — This week, President Donald Trump drew criticism when he announced via Twitter that he had given his Press Secretary, Sarah Huckabee Sanders, permission to stop doing press briefings from the White House. Trump cited the press treating Ms. Huckabee Sanders "rudely & inaccurately" in a tweet.

This morning a reporter from *The Los Angeles Tribune* happened to come upon the president as he returned back to the White House from his routine doughnut/coffee/nacho cheese dipped pretzel/KFC/McDonald's run. She asked him if he thinks it's fair that Huckabee Sanders collect her salary — which is roughly $180,000 — for not working, especially while there are almost a million furloughed government employees not getting a paycheck during the government shutdown he proudly told Sen. Chuck Schumer (D-NY) and Speaker of the House Nancy Pelosi (D-CA) he would take the blame for last month.

Trump admitted the reporter had a "point" but he dismissed it entirely.

"I dismiss that question entirely," Trump said, waving what looked

JANUARY

like a baby hand poking out from the over-sized black duster that he wears even indoors, to look slimmer and trim. "The bottom line is that I had to shut the government down to get my monument — er I mean — for border security. And besides, everyone kept complaining that all Sarah does is lie all the time, and keeping her from going out there was literally the only way to keep her from lying."

White House doctors confirmed that what Trump said is true.

"We've been over and over Sarah's charts, and she's definitely got a very rare condition," Dr. Brook James told the media. "She's got Gumflapitis, which presents with symptoms that include: making terrible jokes only you and your corpulent father thinks are funny, smoky eyes, and the inability to open one's mouth without lies spewing out."

Reached for comment, former Press Secretary Sean Spicer gave kudos to both Trump and Sanders.

"This is the smartest way to look innocent, period," Spicer said. "In no way does it look like, to normal, intelligent people, that they're hiding stuff, or that they literally are incapable of telling the American people the truth, period. Also, Donald Trump can fly and Sarah Huckabee Sanders doesn't even like nacho cheese, period."

JANUARY 31, 2019

God Denies Any Collusion With Trump Campaign

HEAVEN — God has issued a statement distancing herself from the Donald Trump presidential administration.

"Um. No. I didn't pick that douche. But LOL to anyone who thinks I would," God's letter states very plainly. "I don't pick presidents as a matter of principle and standard operating procedure. But I can assure you that a guy who doesn't in any way, shape, or form represent even the most basic of my New Testament teachings wouldn't even remotely come close to getting my endorsement, if I was prone to do such a thing, which, again, I am not."

Ms. God writes that she was "compelled" to make this historic statement by Trump's Press Secretary, Sarah Huckabee Sanders' claims in an interview with the Christian Broadcasting Network that God had "wanted Donald Trump to become president." The statements made by Huckabee were so out of step with reality, God says, that she had no choice but to break with longstanding precedent and weigh in from her deified position on a matter of mortal politics.

"We do things the new school way now, but even if we were still hardcore Old Testament, can Sarah say with a straight face that her boss

JANUARY

even follows half of the Ten Commandments," God asked rhetorically. "The man bears false witness sixteen times before he gets out of bed in the morning. And even though I didn't say it specifically, coveting thy son-in-law's piece of ass isn't very Christian or Godly either, folks."

God states unequivocally that she doesn't get involved in any political race.

"Is Sarah really so dumb? By her rationale, I also would have put Obama in office, too. Or does she think I gave you all Obama so you could get Trump," God scoffed. "That's beyond stupid. I mean, I know I'm the one who murdered every life form on Earth with a flood because I was feeling like no one was paying me enough attention, but even I know that going from Obama to Trump is like going from a BMW to getting punched in the dick and diarrhea in the face after you get out of a BMW."

Even though she would not ever endorse a single candidate, God did say that she's seen some people who fit her ideal candidate's description.

"But he's already been president, is over 90 years old, has beaten cancer a couple times, and is too busy building homes for the poor — you know, being a real Christian — and you all took him for granted the first time around anyway," God writes. "But no, I wouldn't pick the guy who is terrible to refugees when my own son was a religious refugee, for my sake!"

The White House responded by calling God "fake news" and said a suit would be filed in court shortly to declare the president acting God.

FEBRUARY

FEBRUARY 4, 2019

President's Plane Renamed "Air Force Individual-1"

WASHINGTON, D.C. — President Donald Trump's aircraft has been officially rechristened.

"Because Special Counsel Robert Mueller's investigation is ongoing, and because it seems every couple of weeks he's arresting and indicting someone even closer to the president and his inner circle, we thought it best to be on the safe side and rename his plan Air Force Individual-1," announced the Secret Service and Air Force in a joint statement.

At the end of last year, President Trump's former personal attorney Michael Cohen was arrested and subsequently indicted on a bevy of charges stemming from hush money he paid to women on behalf of then-candidate Trump. In the sentencing agreement, Mueller's office lays out that Cohen, at the direction of someone the papers only refer to as "Individual-1," lied to Congress about Trump Tower projects in Moscow that the president claimed were not being pursued. In labeling the president as "Individual-1," Mueller evoked memories in many of Richard Nixon, the last sitting president to be an unnamed co-conspirator in a series of crimes prosecuted by a special counselor.

A LITTLE BIT LOUDER AND A WHOLE LOT WORSE

"The president likes to have consistent branding on everything that he's involved with," Press Secretary Sarah Huckabee Sanders briefed reporters from the White House test kitchens, where she was eating a batch of nacho cheese dipped chocolate chip cookie dough with her bare hands. "Renaming his official presidential aircraft to something that most Americans most identify with him seems to be a pretty genius stroke if you ask me."

In addition to a name change, the president's airplane will also undergo more changes this coming year.

"We're changing the in-flight menu to be exclusively McDonald's since that's now the official food sponsor of all White House-related events," Huckabee told reporters. "We'll also be locking the cabin doors so that the president's sons Eric and Don Jr. stop asking the pilots if they can 'drive like Daddy' lets them drive their family yacht."

The president is said to be mostly okay with this change.

"He's not even sure how much longer Vlad's going to let him be president anyway," one source close to the situation told us. "So, he's kinda like, whatever man, you know?"

FEBRUARY 6, 2019

Trump Tells Secret Service to Investigate Pelosi's 'Threatening Sarcastic Clapping'

WASHINGTON, D.C. — Last night, President Donald Trump gave the second State of the Union address of his presidency.

Unsurprisingly, Mr. Trump repeatedly emphasized his case for a border wall, the funding for which has been the subject of rancorous and unending debate within the federal government. When the Democrats took back control of the House last year, it ensured that the border wall fight would continue, and the government even underwent a partial shutdown at the end of last year, which continued into this year. The shutdown even caused Speaker of the House Nancy Pelosi to postpone the State of the Union speech over security and funding concerns.

Trump's address lasted about an hour and a half, and while it wasn't as bombastic as his campaign rallies were during the 2016 presidential election or last year's midterms, it still had plenty of moments for Trump to ramp up his rhetoric. At one point, Trump defiantly announced that the United States would "never" be a socialist country. While the speech went generally without any major incident — in past years Republican congressional members have shouted at former

A LITTLE BIT LOUDER AND A WHOLE LOT WORSE

President Obama, for instance — there was one series of events that transpired last night which reportedly has the president in a lather.

"This morning, the president directed the Secret Service to interview and investigate Speaker of the House Nancy Pelosi to determine if assault charges can be brought for her horrific, violent, caustic, and threatening sarcastic clapping," Press Secretary Sarah Huckabee Sanders yelled at reporters on the White House lawn. "We're not even sure if sarcastic clapping is covered under the Second Amendment, let alone the First. Speaker Pelosi's actions posed a direct threat to the president...'s ego and pride."

Huckabee explained that President Trump didn't "make a big deal" out of the moment at the time because he doesn't "get sarcasm at the moment."

"Doctors have explained it to us. Basically, it takes a certain level of intellect to detect sarcasm in real-time," Huckabee said. "Despite the president having the best, bigliest, and smartest brain in the whole wide world, and of any president, especially previous black ones, the president simply doesn't have the intelligence he'd need to pick up on the sarcasm in Speaker Pelosi's clapping."

One of the first items on Trump's published agenda today was re-watching the address. Huckabee reported that the president likes to start every day looking at tape of himself. Trump likes to have a container of warm tapioca pudding next to him while he watches the tape of himself. He also likes to be without pants, Huckabee said.

When Trump watched the footage, he was outraged to find out that

FEBRUARY

Pelosi's clapping didn't seem very sincere. That's when he decided that he had been personally attacked by Pelosi's sarcastic response to his call for an end to bitter, divisive politics. Trump had just lashed out on Twitter at Democrats hours before making such a declaration during his address. Huckabee says that when he decided he'd been attacked, Trump knew he had to get the Secret Service involved.

"She knows how unintelligent the president is, from first-hand interactions with him," Sanders explained, "so this was clearly a direct attack on one of his biggest weaknesses — his complete and total stupidity."

Speaker Pelosi, reached for comment, said she'd respond to Trump "in due time," but that she had to first put his testicles back away and get her foot out of his rectum, which it has been lodged up since she won the shutdown fight and reopened the government without any border wall funding.

"Don can literally fuck off, like for reals," Pelosi said, laughing uncontrollably. "Like, he can fuck all the way off to Fuck Off Town and drive the Fuck Off bus to the center of Fuck Off Square and then go fuck himself, publicly. Oh, sorry, there I go being sarcastic again. I better stop before Donny tries to drop a nuke on Fuck Off Town."

This is a developing story.

FEBRUARY 14, 2019

Trump: It's 'Treasonous' That Andrew McCabe and Others Put Country Ahead of Loyalty to Him

WASHINGTON, D.C. — An explosive new "60 Minutes" interview and a new book from former FBI Director Andrew McCabe is lighting the Hill on fire, and it has President Trump very angry.

During the interview, McCabe confirms that he opened up obstruction of justice probes on Trump for firing James Comey. Trump had admitted to Lester Holt in an interview on NBC that he'd fired Comey over the Russia investigation. This was a red flag to McCabe, who also said he believed current FBI Director Rod Rosenstein was actually serious about offering to wear a wire and record conversations with Trump. One more, final explosive detail in the interview and book is that several DOJ officials considered checking with Trump's cabinet to get a pulse on who would support removing the president by way of the 25th amendment, which is supposed to act as a measure by which a president can be removed if he is incapable of performing the job duties of the presidency.

Trump took to Twitter and bashed McCabe, a frequent target of his ire.

As livid as Trump was on Twitter, sources within the White House

FEBRUARY

are reporting that in the Oval Office Trump was absolutely unhinged and beside himself with anger at McCabe.

"You're telling me he was concerned for his country and took his oath to defend it so seriously he investigated the situation to determine a course of action? He's a fucking REPUBLICAN," Trump screamed. "Doesn't he realize I'm a Republican too?! If it's not treason to put your country ahead of your party, I don't know what is!"

President Trump wasn't sure if he was having the right reaction to this news. There was someone who could help him determine if he was correct in assuming McCabe was being treasonous. The president picked up the phone, where his secretary answered.

"Hi. Get me, Vlad, on the Kushner Back Channel right now! This is a real national emergency we're dealing with, more so than 8.2 trillion illegal Mexican-ish people in caravans, even," Trump shouted.

After a few tense and nervous moments, Putin came on the line.

"Vlad! How are you, sir? Good, good. Hey, look, boss, I gotta question for you," Trump greeted Putin. "Is Andy McCabe being a total cuck traitor right now? Because I'm pretty sure he is, but I know you're the one who would know for sure."

Putin started talking.

"Uh-huh. Yeah. Yup. Exactly. Oh yeah, we shredded those. And those. Mmhmm. Thanks, Mr. Putin. I knew I could count on you to point me in the right direction."

Trump hung up and dialed another number.

"Mitch! Mitch baby! How's my favorite reptile? Cool, cool,"

A LITTLE BIT LOUDER AND A WHOLE LOT WORSE

Trump said to Senate Majority Leader Mitch McConnell. "Hey, Mitchy baby. Quick question for you. It's like, the worst crime imaginable for someone to betray us, right?"

McConnell asked Trump something.

"Right, the Republican Party is the us I'm talking about, exactly," Trump responded. McConnell started saying something back. "Yeah, that's what I thought. McCabe is a total loser-ass loser who loses, like his stupid-ass wife. Man, why do people think I'm just a big baby and bully? Anyway, thanks a lot Mitch, love you. Kisses to the baby turtles. Peace!"

At the time of publication, Trump was in a meeting with the Presidents of Puerto Rico and Mississippi, determining if Space Force should be called up to active duty to neutralize McCabe as soon as possible. It's unclear at this time what advice the other two presidents are giving Trump.

This is a developing story.

FEBRUARY 21, 2019

Mexico Agrees to Pay for National Emergency as Long as Trump Can Prove It Exists

MEXICO CITY, MEXICO — The Federal Government of Mexico has sent an official communique to both houses of Congress, offering to shoulder the financial burden of "any national emergency that Trump can prove is real."

"To the people of the United States of America and its duly elected Congress (not their highly-suspiciously elected so-called "president")," the Mexican letter opens, "We, the people of Mexico, wish to officially offer you any financial assistance you require to pay for the current national emergency along our northern, your southern, border. Provided, of course, your alleged president can offer proof of its existence."

Earlier this month, Trump declared a national emergency over funding for his promised border wall. Throughout the 2016 presidential campaign, however, Trump promised that Mexico would pay for the wall. Despite the spin that a renegotiated NAFTA trade deal would provide funding for the wall from Mexico's tariffs and taxes from the pact, the fact remains that to this day Mexico has remained steadfast in its denials of that request.

A LITTLE BIT LOUDER AND A WHOLE LOT WORSE

"In fact, not only will the people of Mexico pay for all the costs associated with this current national emergency, we will foot the bill for any national emergency during the Trump presidency," Mexico wrote. "Provided, of course, that Mr. Trump can provide even a scintilla of evidence to back up any of his claims."

President Trump received a copy of Mexico's letter and reportedly was enraged. The president was so upset he called a hasty press conference but only invited "state-run and/or friendly, positive, NOT FAKE NEWS" sources, as the press release from Sarah Huckabee Sanders' office stated.

FEBRUARY 22, 2019

Kellyanne Conway: National Emergency at Border 'Much Bigger and Worser Crisis' Than Bowling Green Massacre

WASHINGTON, D.C. — One of President Trump's most vocal and loyal aides, Kellyanne Conway, was stopped on her way into the White House this morning and asked about several topics. Speaking to reporters for about ten minutes, Conway talked about the Mueller investigation, the Jussie Smollett case, and addressed the ongoing national emergency at the southern border. The president declared an emergency last week in a Rose Garden ceremony.

"We're all looking forward to seeing and immediately shredding the Mueller report because if you don't see it, it doesn't exist," Conway told reporters. "We're also planning on sticking our fingers in our ears and humming loudly, as well as closing our eyes super tight. That way when they come and knock on our door in the morning, we don't have to get arrested because it'll be like the FBI isn't even there!"

Conway said that Smollett proves "libtards are the crazy ones, not patriotic MAGA boys."

"I was just talking to Cesar Sayoc, you know, the MAGA bomber? And he said that it's just nuts how Jussie would try to imply MAGA lovers are violent," Conway said, "and the Proud Boys backed him up

A LITTLE BIT LOUDER AND A WHOLE LOT WORSE

on that!"

On the subject of the ongoing crisis at the southern border, Conway said that the emergency is not only "completely and totally real" it's also "very much so not fake" as well as "definitely not just made up because the president got real sad that Congress wasn't his little bitches anymore."

"The bottom line here, guys, is that this crisis is very real," Conway said. "In fact, it's a much bigger and worse crisis than even the Bowling Green Massacre! There are for more lives at stake in this emergency, and believe me, I watched the Bowling Green Massacre on our network of microwave TV cameras. I know how devastating that all was."

Ms. Conway said that the border crisis "might even be worse than Benghazi."

"Benghazi was, of course, the worst tragedy in American history. I confirmed that with Chinese, Irish, and Mexican immigrants, as well as with some uppity urbanites who still think racism is a thing, and of course with a couple of redskins — excuse me, Native Indians," Conway declared. "They all agreed this is, like, much worse, fam."

Conway indicated that the president is not worried about a scheduled vote on the House floor next week that would officially block his emergency declaration. The "privileged" resolution will be taken up next Tuesday and is expected to easily pass the House. Whether or not enough Republicans in the Senate vote for it depends on how many of them feel their constituents are behind Trump's power grab or not.

"If they pass that resolution, we'll either veto it or Vladimir Putin

FEBRUARY

will," Conway said. "One way or another someone who's in charge of the executive branch will veto it. So yeah, whatever, and stuff, you know what I mean?"

FEBRUARY 27, 2019

Courier Hands Cohen Check Signed by President Trump Just Before Entering Capitol Building

WASHINGTON, D.C. — The collective political world is at a standstill, waiting with great anticipation the public congressional testimony from Michael Cohen, President Donald Trump's longtime former personal attorney. Mr. Cohen is expected to testify to moments of Trump's racism, as well as to details that implicate Trump in crimes committed both before and after taking office.

Mr. Trump is currently in Vietnam, meeting with the autocratic dictator Kim Jong-Un of North Korea. In a tweet, Trump tried to distance himself from Cohen, as well as cast doubts on his trustworthiness.

President Trump's tweet surprised hardly anyone on the Hill. It has long since been a part of his persona to attack people he sees as a threat to him. That Cohen is also someone who has turned on Trump probably rankled the president even more than usual. But in a stunning turn of events, it would appear that Trump is attempting to change tactics at the 11th hour.

Moments before Mr. Cohen entered the capitol building, set to testify before a House committee, a courier stopped him. A plain

FEBRUARY

envelope was handed to Mr. Cohen, who promptly opened it. Inside the envelope was a check for $130,000 and a hand-written note on presidential stationery.

"Dear Mickey Coham or Whatever Your Name Is (I Barely Know You, Of Course)," Trump's letter reads. "I figured you always lie when I pay you, so now would be a good time for you to start lying for me again. Please, if you can remember to do so, lie for me again. Accept this money on behalf of the entire Trump Crime Syndicate. It's for you, provided you keep your dirty rat mouth shut, Mickey!"

The letter is particular in what Trump wants Cohen to lie about.

"Instead of confirming that I'm a racist white-collar crook," Trump writes, "do the opposite. Do un-that, Mickey. Do it for me, one more time, for old crimes' sake!"

Cohen immediately handed the check to FBI Special Counsel Robert Mueller, who happened to be on a leisurely stroll when he saw the commotion with the courier.

"Thanks, Mike. I'll put this check and the letter on top of all the tweets we've printed out," Mueller said. "I would have never guessed that I'd be mounting a criminal case against a sitting president 280 characters at a time, but here are…face to face… a couple of Silver Spoons."

Cohen and Mueller sang a small bit from the "Silver Spoons" theme song as a duet.

"Together! We're gonna find our way! Together! Taking the time each day," Cohen sang.

A LITTLE BIT LOUDER AND A WHOLE LOT WORSE

"To learn all about, those things you just can't buy," Mueller sang back.

"Two silver spoons together," Cohen sang again.

"You and I," they sang together.

Mr. Cohen shook Mueller's hand and bade him farewell.

FEBRUARY 28, 2019

Jim Jordan Shreds Cohen Testimony: 'Total Waste of Taxpayer Dollars' That 'Didn't Get Into Benghazi Even Once'

WASHINGTON, D.C. — Rep. Gym Jordan told a right-wing talk radio station today that the hearing held before the House Oversight and Reform Committee yesterday was a "total waste of taxpayer dollars." Jordan said because no one asked Michael Cohen, President Donald Trump's former personal attorney, and fixer, any questions about the 2012 terror attack in Benghazi, Libya.

"Let me ask you this, why did Michael Cohen not once get into his involvement with the Benghazi affair? Is he covering up for Hillary Clinton or Barack Obama? We might not ever know," Jordan told W-KKK's Chet Chitterson during the afternoon drive time. "And that's just a shame. A total and complete farce, if you ask me."

Yesterday marked the first time that Democrats have had a chance to convene the oversight committee for a hearing on the 2016 presidential election, and any collusion with the Russian government perpetrated by the Trump campaign. FBI Special Counsel Robert Mueller's investigation is still ongoing, but for the last two years, House Dems have had to settle for being sidelined players as the minority party in the House. With the Republicans being shellacked in last year's

A LITTLE BIT LOUDER AND A WHOLE LOT WORSE

mid-terms and losing 40 seats, the Democrats have been able to rest the gavel from the GOP's hands, and now are holding their own hearings.

"I just can't understand for the life of me why we're discussing anything *but* Benghazi, or at least some other scandal involving Democrats," Jordan howled. "I mean, some of us on our side of the aisle have gotten used to how things were. We like our traditions; we're conservatives after all. And, traditionally, this committee has only investigated the burps, farts, sniffles, sneezes, and coughs of Democrats named Clinton or Obama. Now all of a sudden we're supposed to care about actual crimes being committed in the Oval Office? Poppycock, I say!"

Jordan then recalled that "Peeper Cock" was what his nickname on the college wrestling team was.

"And another thing, why are we talking to a liar in this committee," Jordan asked rhetorically. "We already got a liar in the Oval Office, and I'm a small-government Republican, so it seems like wasteful big government spending to haul another liar into congress if you ask me."

Rep. Jordan was extremely upset that he and his fellow Freedom Caucus member Rep. Mark Meadows of North Carolina "put a lot of hard work into coming up with distractions" from Cohen's testimony, and the press didn't report on them enough. Jordan says that it's a "miscarriage of justice" for Cohen to "give us corroborating evidence like some kind of libtard."

"But what really gets my goat is that we spent hours meticulously making the case for why Cohen is a liar who can't be trusted," Jordan

FEBRUARY

told Chitterson, "and all the lamestream media can talk about is how we basically proved that Trump's a liar who needs liars to work for him so they can do his lying for him. What the friggin' H, man?! All that work for nothing!"

Jordan says that even if Cohen had somehow implied that Trump was involved with Benghazi, that would have satisfied his personal criteria for a successful and newsworthy hearing.

"I mean, shit, throw us a bone, Michael! Imply Trump's mixed up with Killary and Benghazi, I don't know," Jordan said, sputtering but with emotional sincerity. "Maybe I'm just a little lost and heartbroken at these hearings now that I can't just bloviate non-stop to run out the clock on holding Trump accountable. Maybe I just need to go hit the showers. I don't know."

Jordan would have been happy if any number of Obama or Clinton era scandals had been discussed.

"Would it have killed them to ask Cohen a single question about what he knew about Whitewater? Vince Foster? Anything? Jeez, talk about abdicating your responsibilities," Jordan quipped. "They didn't even ask once about Jade Helm or Obama's FEMA gay frog chemtrail camps! I tried to ask about him taking 'In God We Trust' off our money and coins, and I was cut off because I ran out of time!"

The Freedom Caucus has decided that they will pursue the Benghazi/Cohen angle themselves, without the support of the oversight committee.

"We will leave no stone unturned, no pussy un-grabbed, no piss

A LITTLE BIT LOUDER AND A WHOLE LOT WORSE

whore un-Russia'd," Jordan said, "until we get to the bottom of what Hillary Clinton brainwashed Donald Trump's longtime personal lawyer into doing on behalf of her, George Soros, Saul Alinsky, and Osama Bin Barack Obama, or we'll die watching naked boys shower and also probably trying!"

This is a developing story.

MARCH

MARCH 5, 2019

Trump: 'I Didn't Obstruct Justice, I Just Tried to Impede an Investigation!'

WASHINGTON, D.C. — Today, President Donald Trump lashed out the media, Democrats, and Special Counsel Robert Mueller and he explained that he knows "deep, deep down" that he didn't commit obstruction of justice.

"There is no friggin' way I committed any obstruction of justice," Trump tweeted, "that's just FAKE NEWS lies."

Mr. Trump explained in a series of tweets that it was "impossible" for him to have obstructed justice because he hadn't even heard of that term up until the point that he became president. Now, two years into Mueller's investigation, when it appears that Congressional Democrats are also going to start pursuing an investigation into whether Trump committed obstruction of justice during Mueller's probe of the 2016 presidential election.

"I didn't obstruct any justice," Trump reiterated, "that's just not my style. And even if it was, which it might be, who knows, I had never even heard of that phrase until that jerk ass Mueller came around getting all high and mighty on me. I mean, who appointed him special prosecutor?"

A LITTLE BIT LOUDER AND A WHOLE LOT WORSE

The president tried to spell out in very simple terms exactly what he thought he had done, instead of obstructing justice.

"I didn't obstruct justice," Trump tweeted, "I just tried to impede an investigation into one of my comrades. The FAKE NEWS needs to get over this!"

Trump tried to plead ignorance, as well.

"How could I do something without knowing what it is," Trump asked, adding, "That doesn't make sense. It's like saying I can break the speed limit when I don't know what it is on that particular stretch of highway."

The president explained that even if Americans "don't buy the ignorance of the law thing," there are plenty of other compelling reasons to see he's innocent.

"Folks, the bottom line that the mainstream FAKE NEWS MEDIA won't tell you," Trump tweeted, "is that I didn't obstruct justice, period. My lawyers tell me that, and I pay them good money to tell me things I want to know."

Neither Special Counselor Mueller nor the Department of Justice could not be reached for comment.

MARCH 7, 2019

Trump Regrets Lying About Lying About Telling Michael Cohen to Lie About Him Lying

WASHINGTON, D.C. — When Donald Trump came down from the White House's presidential residence to the Oval Office late this afternoon to retrieve a copy of *TV Guide* he'd left on the Resolute Desk, he was surprised to find a handful of reporters milling about. Trump invited them into the office and gave an impromptu, fifteen-minute press conference. Understandably, the focus of most of the reporters' questions was the testimony of Michael Cohen, Mr. Trump's once longtime personal attorney and "fixer."

During a hearing of the House Oversight Committee, Cohen testified that Trump is a "racist," and gave the committee copies of checks signed by the president himself. The checks were purported by Cohen to represent repayment for the hush money he laid out on Trump's behalf to adult film star Stormy Daniels in the waning days of the 2016 presidential election. Cohen was indicted and plead guilty to several counts stemming from FBI Special Counsel Robert Mueller's investigation into the Trump campaign and Russian interference in the election.

Trump was asked if he has any regrets about anything related to

A LITTLE BIT LOUDER AND A WHOLE LOT WORSE

Cohen, or his tenure as the president's attorney. Though he isn't one that's known for self-reflection and holding himself accountable, Mr. Trump did admit to harboring at least some feelings of regret when it comes to Michael Cohen.

"Regrets? I've got a few, sure," Trump admitted. "I regret, with the gift of hiney-sight, ever lying about lying about telling Michael Cohen to lie about how I lied. That was just, frankly, one lie too many. And it's like that scene in *A Christmas Story*, with all the plugs in the outlet? One lie too many and it blows the whole thing out."

The president then mentally worked out, out loud, where exactly he went wrong, in his own estimation.

"I think if I had only lied about the first lies that I told, but lied about the lies I told Mickey Coham to tell for me about the lies that I told, then I'd have been just fine," Trump suggested. "Then again, if I had just merely lied about lying about the lies that I told, but let him lie his own lies about the lies I told him to lie about the lies I lied about instead of letting him lie his own lies, then I'd probably also be okay."

Now Trump was really going.

"But! What if I had told an untruth about a lie about a fib that was to cover-up a mendacity that I had Mickey Coham tell as part of a bigger lie that Vlad told me to tell so that no one remembered I lied about lying about lying about telling Coham to lie," Trump barreled on, losing breath. "Yeah, that's probably it."

Trump snapped his fingers. He'd thought of yet another different scenario he should have tried.

MARCH

"Oh! If I had told the truth about lying about lying about telling him to lie about him lying," Trump said, "that's how I'd have come away from this whole thing cleanly! I knew I'd find it. I was so close, before, too."

Trump farted and instinctively blamed Sarah Huckabee Sanders, who was not in the room at the time.

"Stinky Sarah, eh folks? Right? That's what I call her behind her back. Anyway," Trump said, "who can blame me for getting so confused, huh? So much lying and double-lying on top of more lying. What's a senile old pill snortin' fake billionaire and faker president supposed to do? Who knew a web of lies covering up decades of financial crimes both in and out of office was so complicated?"

MARCH 9, 2019

Trump Asked Woman If the Bible He Signed is 'Any Good or Not'

FT. CONFEDERATE, ALABAMA — Yesterday, President Donald Trump visited the State of Alabama in the wake of a series of absolutely harrowing and devastating tornadoes. Trump tweeted last week that he'd directed FEMA to give Alabama "A-plus" treatment, and visiting the state was a top priority for him as soon as his bone spur swelling went down enough for his spine to grow back.

During his visit, Trump was seen greeting survivors and their loved ones. Perhaps in a bit of a peculiar development, while in an evangelical church, Trump was seen taking bibles from people and autographing them. Reportedly, one such bible has already been sold on eBay for an astounding $666. Today, we learned that while Trump was signing another Alabaman's bible, he asked her for her a review of it.

"Hey, lemme ask you, something sweetheart, since we're both here and I'm signing this thing for you," Trump said to the woman. "Is this thing any good or not? It's super heavy, has a lot of words, and no pictures. I didn't even know you could have a book without pictures, but apparently, you can? I think we may have to look into opening up those laws though because it seems unfair to people named Trump to expect

MARCH

them to read words. Don Jr. hasn't read a single word all by himself his entire life, and he dictates his tweets to a chicken we get drunk and have just peck the keys because that chicken is technically smarter than he is."

Trump swirled a silver sharpie over the cover of the bible, inscribing it with his signature.

"I've always meant to read the thing," Trump told the white evangelical Christian woman in front of him. "I just never had the time. And again, NO PICTURES in the whole thing! I mean, who am I to second-guess God, right? But then again, I'm the president and he's not, right? So, hey, maybe God, if that's even his real name, should take a couple pointers from me. I am pretty much considered, and people who I promise to pay money to always are telling me this, one of the most bestest communicating people out there."

The woman started to reach out for her bible, but Trump just kept talking to her for some reason.

"Marketing genius, they tell me, all the time. Well, stable marketing genius, always stable. Very stable. Make sure you go home and tell all your friends and family," Trump said, jabbing his finger in the direction of the woman's face. Had it been longer, he may have poked her nose. "Okay? Stable. Marketing. Genius. And at any rate, I really think God should consider putting a couple pictures in there."

The president pressed on, not noticing that the woman had checked the time on her phone twice and had started rotating her wrist and in a traditional "hurry it the hell up" fashion.

A LITTLE BIT LOUDER AND A WHOLE LOT WORSE

"Ooh! Oooh! You know Ivanka, can I call you Ivanka? I find that if I just call every female Ivanka it works out really well for me because I have to remember way fewer names," Trump said. "Anyhow, Ivanka, you know that magazine, *Playboy?* Great magazine. I gave Hef the idea to do it, actually. Don't look that up. But I did. He's dead so he can't deny it, just remember that. Anyway, God should go that route. Put in maybe some pictures of fine ladies, shall we say, other Ivankas, if you will. That would spice up sales, I bet."

Trump just kept going.

"Does the bible even sell that well, to begin with? I bet it doesn't sell as many copies as my book," Trump wondered. "Anyway, Ivanka, they tell me, I think it's in Two Corinthians, that praying is like calling up God on the phone. Maybe next time you pray you to ask if God wants me to go ahead and make an official Trump Bible with naked ladies in it. Just you know something he should consider."

Finally, the president handed the woman back her bible. She would later tell reporters she's now "a bit undecided" in the 2020 race, and will see if the Republican Party puts up any primary challengers before she commits. President Trump was still signing bibles.

A small child handed him her youth edition bible. Trump's jaw dropped. He started turning around and showing everyone in his Secret Service detail and personal entourage the bible. It had pictures on it. Lots and lots of pictures.

"Sweetheart, do you mind if I keep this, you don't mind," Trump asked and answered himself in one run-on question. "I'll send you an

MARCH

autographed copy of my book in the mail. Give your address to this guy here, okay? You'll like it way more than this, and I promise you'll learn a lot. I know I did when they told me the guy I paid to write it for me was done. Okay, vote Trump, you have no choice, byeeeeeeeeeeeeee!"

Trump was ushered away out of the church, and into an awaiting limousine. The White House estimates the president will have completed reading the picture book bible by the end of his first presidential term, or hopefully, his permanent prison term.

This story is developing.

MARCH 22, 2019

J.K. Rowling Says You Didn't Actually Read Harry Potter Novels

LONDONSHERRY DOWNTONSHIRE, ENGLAND — Author J.K. Rowling has quite a close, intimate relationship with the characters that inhabit the universe of Harry Potter. This makes sense, considering Rowling is the woman who invented Potter and his friends, and the entire "wizarding world" that they inhabit. Since the final book in the original series was published over a decade ago, Rowling has made a few tweaks and additions to the canon of the story, such as announcing that Dumbledore the Wizard and headmaster at Hogwarts was, in fact, a member of the LGBT community.

Now, Rowling has come out and made her the boldest change to the stories yet.

"I'm sorry to say that you didn't actually read the Harry Potter stories," Rowling said in a tweet. "You were not reading a story about a boy who found out he had magical powers. You did not read a story about the magical universe he inhabits, and you did not read seven separate novels that told a long, beautiful narrative about the boy growing up and realizing a destiny all his own."

Rowling continued to explain herself in a series of tweets.

MARCH

"I've decided that I didn't actually write those books. They never existed. Sure, you might have memories. Those memories might even be of stories that feel an awful lot like my Harry Potter stories," Rowling tweeted. "Let me assure you — you didn't do any of that. You were all actually reading a story about a mouse with a big dream, and the whacky adventures she has on her way to the Big City, where she plans to cure cancer, ride on a rocket to Mars, and eventually become the first female mouse intercontinental balloonist to win the Indy 500!"

Ms. Rowling says that she will always have "an affinity and true love" for the characters of the Harry Potter universe, but that she also suffers from a rare condition that keeps her from simply starting a new artistic endeavor to address anything she feels she missed in an earlier work and instead forces her to keep cramming new stuff into her old books.

"I have been diagnosed with GeorgeLucasism, a rare but tragic condition that prevents artists from accepting that a piece of work they completed is finished, and they need to start new works of art," Rowling said. "I imagine I'll be tinkering at the edges of the Harry Potter — excuse me, Henrietta the Mighty Martian Mouse — novels until I draw my last breath here on Earth."

MARCH 28, 2019

White Nationalism Ban Briefly Brings Down President's Facebook Page

SWILLYCORN VALLEY, CALIFORNIA — This week, Facebook announced sweeping new policy changes in an effort to curb the use of their platform by purveyors of hate speech, issuing a permanent ban of white nationalist and white separatist content. This year, Republican Congressman Steve King of Iowa was stripped of all his committee assignments when during an interview he asked why the term "white nationalist" has a bad connotation. In 2018, the FBI reported that almost all of the domestic terror attacks were perpetrated by far-right-wing groups.

Facebook's policy shift is meant to stop groups dedicated to white nationalism and white separatism — also known as white supremacy groups — from recruiting with their platform. Sources this morning are reporting that just a few hours ago, Facebook's ban on white nationalism brought down two pages.

"This morning, at approximately 3:15am, as President Trump was on another social media site using his Executive Time to troll a 19-year-old standup comic who made fun of him in a YouTube clip of his set, the official Facebook pages for Donald J. Trump and the White House

MARCH

were temporary unpublished," Facebook's CEO and head automaton Mark Zuckerberg announced in a blog post. "This was done erroneously, and we have restored the pages."

Zuckerberg's blog post says that "while the White House page and Trump's personal page" have become "cesspools of lies and white nationalism," it's not his company's policy, in general, to unpublish or ban heads of state.

"This is a tricky situation. Is Donald Trump a racist white nationalist reality-TV conman? Of course," Zuckerberg writes. "But he's also, somehow, beyond all logic and reason, the current President of the United States of America. So we kinda have to thread a needle, in terms of how much of his content we block or takedown."

Mr. Zuckerberg acknowledges that even if Facebook had kept Trump's page and the White House page down, there would still be "lots and lots of racists" on his site.

"The question we are grappling with is how we respect free speech but also keep racism off," Zuckerberg wrote. "One person suggested permabanning anyone who changed their middle name to 'Benghazi' on Facebook. Some others have suggested simply doing a search for people who have MAGA hats on in their profile, but our algorithm couldn't distinguish between MAGA hats and klan hoods, despite the coloring differences, so we scrapped that idea."

For now, the pages will stay published, and Zuckerberg has issued an apology to the White House.

"It's not that there is an absolute ton of white nationalist rhetoric

A LITTLE BIT LOUDER AND A WHOLE LOT WORSE

coming from those pages, it's that we're not sure how to handle one of our biggest, most racist trolls also happening to be the most powerful person in the free world," Zuckerberg wrote. "But we are sorry if we hurt the president's feelings, which we all know are his top priority to protect."

APRIL

APRIL 11, 2019

Barr Investigating If Obama Administration Forced Trump to Be Lifelong Lying Conman and Racist Idiot

WASHINGTON, D.C. — Earlier this year, during Senate testimony, William Barr — Attorney General and designer of President Trump's latest model of handbags designed to carry water for as long is as necessary — sent shock waves through the Hill when he said he believed "spying did occur" on the Trump campaign in 2016. Barr would later walk back just how forcefully he was making the claim, though he said he was trying to get his "arms around" everything that transpired in the Mueller investigation.

Barr said he thinks it's a "big problem" when campaigns spied on.

It has long been asserted without any evidence by Trump that the Obama administration spied on his campaign. However, even the last attorney general stopped short of ever accusing the Obama White House of malfeasance, and in fact, in the two years since taking office, the theory that Obama "spied" on Trump has been shot down by officials in both political parties. Whatever Barr's impetus for opening the new investigation, apparently he isn't content to just open one; Barr is opening another investigation into the Obama administration.

"What I think everyone, every single American citizen, wants to

A LITTLE BIT LOUDER AND A WHOLE LOT WORSE

know is something very simple," Barr told reporters coming back from his lunch break today, "and that's whether or not the previous presidential administration did anything to force the current president to be a duplicitous, lifelong conman and racist idiot. I will not rest until these questions are answered."

Barr reiterated that the Mueller Report, which he still has not released, "completely and totally exonerates" Trump on the issue of obstruction of justice. However, it doesn't get into whether or not Barack Obama held a gun to Trump's head and turned him into a lying, double-dealing, corrupt, senile old bastard. That, Barr said, is "of utmost concern" to the security of the nation.

There's no way of knowing how long Obama might have been forcing Trump to be a "literal racist fucking moron." Obviously, Barr argues, it's Obama's fault that there are things about President Trump that are "repugnant and repulsive beyond what Mueller could have ever reported on." Barr knows "deep in [his] heart," that Trump is innocent of charges of obstruction of justice, but he reiterated that the American public cannot see the report that completely exonerates Trump because "it's almost too exonerate-y."

"We know for a fact that Obama personally spied on the president with the microwaves he had installed in the White House before handing over the keys," Barr told reporters. "What I want to know is if he did something earlier, like decades earlier, that made Trump a vile, contemptible piece of human garbage."

AG Barr says there is a "clear and simple" reason he has to

APRIL

investigate Obama.

"Everyone knows Obama is the cause of literally everything that is wrong in America, and frankly the planet," Barr said. "So no we're going to get to the bottom of just how much sway he had on Trump's ability to not be a human racist diatribe in an oversized winter coat."

Ultimately, Barr says there are "just too many unanswered questions" about how Obama treated Trump for him to simply ignore them.

"Did Obama personally force President Trump to say gross things about his daughter? Did Obama personally put a gun to Trump's head and force him to be a tax-dodging liar," Barr asked rhetorically. "If it wasn't Obama, we know it was prolly George Soros or the Clintons, or even the ghost of Saul Alinsky."

Barr brushed aside questions about whether he was wasting taxpayer money investigating a conspiracy theory.

"Excuse me?! Did you not pay attention to the Benghazi hearings? Republicans absolutely love wasting money investigating conspiracy theories," Barr said. "Money is no object. Now, real conspiracies to cover up presidential crimes? That's something Republicans will ignore until, well, forever."

This is a developing story.

APRIL 16, 2019

Barr Exonerates Dozens of Criminals Who Were Arrested After Scooby-Doo's Investigations

WASHINGTON, D.C. — In a truly shocking and unforeseen chain of events, dozens of criminals apprehended by Mystery Incorporated, an independent private investigation firm run by the world's foremost canine detective, have been officially exonerated by Attorney General William Barr. Department of Justice guidelines state that Barr can exonerate, but not commute or terminate, the sentences of almost a hundred different people convicted of committing various crimes, who were all arrested following the work of Mystery Inc.'s Scott "Scooby" Doo, Norville "Shaggy" Rogers, Velma Dinkley, Fred Jones, and Daphne Blake.

"Like, ZOINKS man! I told Scoobs that maybe we should be better about crossing our T's and dotting our I's, but I didn't think we committed any constitutional violations in any of our investigations," Shaggy told us via Skype. "Then again, at the height of our heyday, we were making lots of dough and spending a lot of it on Scooby Snacks, so my memory's definitely gotten a little fuzzy over time."

Barr, at a press conference in front of the Department of Justice, announced that it was his judgment that all of the underlying evidence

APRIL

collected by Scooby and the gang had to be immediately redacted. Barr admitted that from an outsider's point of view, it might look like he's sticking his nose where it doesn't belong. He offered no apologies for that, but instead a short, business-like reasoning.

"The American rubes — excuse me, public — should be used to how Bill Barr rolls by now," Attorney General Barr said. "I want to know who authorized these investigations? We need to investigate the investigators!"

Since 1969, Scooby and the gang have worked as private investigators, attempting to solve mysteries that often involve the spooky and supernatural. Having taken the Elixir of Life at a company picnic in 1972, Scoobs, Shaggy, Daphne, Velma, and Fred haven't aged a day in that time, but have managed to rack up and an impressive string of successfully closed investigations. All of them resulted in the perpetrator being apprehended, or at least that's what everyone assumed before Barr's announcement today.

"Call me crazy, but I want to live in a country where even a ragtag team of hipsters and their talking dog have to follow the law when investigating crimes," Barr said. "I simply want to know under whose authority and under what pretenses all those darn kids started snoopin' around."

Attorney General Barr says he finds it "highly suspicious" that so many of Mystery Inc.'s arrested suspects used a very similar scheme to try and fool authorities.

"Also? Why were so many of the people they caught just wearing rubber masks of other people? Does that really work?" Barr asked, "No, really, President Trump wanted me to ask you guys. Does that work? You know, just in case someone we all know needs to skip town or the country or whatever?"

As ever, Barr said that any and all information he used to inform his judgment "cannot and will not ever" be seen by the public in an unredacted format.

"No, you can't see it. Why would you want to see it? It exonerates them. You can trust me. If I know anything, it's when someone's been exonerated, and buddy, let me tell you," Barr said, "they're all exonerated."

This is a developing story.

APRIL 22, 2019

Trump Shouts 'NO COLLUSION, NO OBSTRUCTION!' in Every Child's Face at White House Egg Roll

WASHINGTON, D.C. — President Donald Trump and Third First Lady Melania Trump hosted the annual White House Easter Egg roll this morning.

It is the third time that Trump has hosted the event, however, it's the first time he's hosted it since the release of the redacted Mueller Report. Though the report painstakingly documented more than ten instances that likely rose to the level of obstruction of justice, FBI Special Counsel Robert Mueller ultimately left the decision to hold Trump accountable for those transgressions to Congress, who has the power to impeach and, perhaps, remove him from office. Attorney General William Barr then interceded and declared that Trump was exonerated completely on charges of obstruction because Mueller was unable to establish a criminal conspiracy.

Mr. Trump was reportedly exuberant this morning as children started arriving for the Easter egg hunt. Trump was so excited, he chose to share his "bigly news" with every kid as they arrived. Trump stood with Third First Lady Melania and greeted each child as they entered the egg roll with a special message.

A LITTLE BIT LOUDER AND A WHOLE LOT WORSE

"NO COLLUSION, NO OBSTRUCTION! YOU HEAR ME, KID?! NO COLLUSION, NO OBSTRUCTION," Trump shouted directly into every child's face. "NO. COLLUSION. NO. OBSTRUCTION."

Trump varied the exact welcome message, but not the tone of urgency, every so often.

"WELCOME TO MY EASTER EGG HUNT! YOU ARE BEING ALLOWED TO HUNT MY EGGS AND WILL HAVE TO GIVE THEM BACK ONCE YOU LEAVE," Trump shouted at one kid. "OH, AND DON'T FORGET — NO OBSTRUCTION! NO COLLUSION! CROOKED H!"

The president told one child that his egg hunt would be "better for the country than Conflicted Bob Mueller's witch hunt that totally and completely exonerated" him.

"NO COLLUSION, LITTLE GIRL! NO COLLUSION! ALSO NO OBSTRUCTION," Trump shouted in a four-year-old girl's face. "YOU MAKE SURE YOU TELL ALL YOUR FRIENDS TO TELL THEIR PARENTS THEY ARE REQUIRED TO VOTE FOR ME CUZ I BEAT BOB MUELLER'S ATTEMPTED COUP THAT TOTALLY AND COMPLETELY EXONERATED ME!"

Attorney General William Barr was in attendance as well. He was seen following President Trump around. Barr was carrying a large bucket of water, and every so often Trump would ask Barr for a drink. That's when Barr would get a big crazy straw out of his jacket and put it into the bucket.

APRIL

"Ah! That's nice! Thanks for carrying my water, Bill," Trump told his attorney general. "But you're prolly getting used to that by now, huh?"

Trump slapped Barr on the back, leaving a tiny KFC grease handprint on his suit jacket.

"Yes, that's right Mr. President. Whatever you say, Mr. President. I'm your personal attorney, of course, Mr. President," Barr told Trump.

As the children filed out from the festivities, Trump handed them each a specially printed card.

"NO COLLUSION! NO OBSTRUCTION!" was printed on each card, with a picture of Trump giving Robert Mueller the finger on the opposite side.

APRIL 23, 2019

Doctors Rushing to Perform Spinal Implants on Congressional Democrats Still on the Fence About Impeaching Trump

WASHINGTON, D.C. — Congressional sources are confirming at the time of publication that a large staff of spinal surgeons has been summoned to the rotunda with a mission to implant spines into as many elected Democrats' bodies as are needed to sufficiently bolster support for impeaching President Donald Trump.

According to reports, capital medical personnel first noticed a potential need for spinal implant surgeries when the Mueller Report, redacted though it is, was released. Doctors say that it became very worrisome to them when they noticed that top Democrats in the House like Reps. Nancy Pelosi and Stenny Hoyer were not willing to push forward on opening impeachment hearings. The Mueller Report states that the team of investigators was unable to establish a criminal conspiracy to collude with Russian operatives, despite having found such evidence. The report also states that because Mueller was bound by the Department of Justice regulations that forbid indicting a sitting president, Congress must act if they wish to hold Trump accountable for the more than instances of obstruction of justice they documented.

"It was all there in black and white, and Mueller made it pretty

APRIL

obvious he'd have been indicting Trump if he thought he could. So it was obviously very concerning for us when Nancy and Stenny started acting like they shouldn't impeach Trump," Dr. Emily Snazback told us.

Snazback is the lead surgeon tasked with assembling a team of doctors that can work around the clock, giving spines to Democrats who need them. Before the Mueller Report was released, Pelosi famously said that it "wasn't worth it" to impeach Trump. Days later, the report was released and it was inescapable that he had at least attempted to severely hamper the investigation, which would seem to rise to the level of obstructing justice. Dr. Snazback says that was a "big red flag" when Pelosi didn't seem even slightly interested in impeaching Trump before the report was released, but it became a "full-blown emergency" when after the release Pelosi still seemed disinterested in impeachment.

"I mean, I don't know how much he has to do to be impeached. I don't think Republicans would need even two counts of possible obstruction to even hold impeachment hearings," Snazback suggested. "So we knew that there might be a major spinal deficiency when more than ten couldn't get Nancy and Stenny moving."

According to Dr. Snazback, it "won't even take that much spine" to initiate impeachment.

"It's literally right there in the Constitution, and Mueller literally told them they can do it," Snazback said. "This is the lowest possible hanging fruit on a tree tipping over with fruit. It's amazing to me that they haven't figured out that a big reason they were swept into office in

A LITTLE BIT LOUDER AND A WHOLE LOT WORSE

the majority in 2018's midterms was that people knew we could impeach Trump easier that way."

Senate Republicans will be getting spinal implants, as well. However, Snazback says it's a "far more urgent matter to the Republic" that Democrats get them first. The impeachment process constitutionally has to begin in the House, and that Snazback says, is why Dems get priority over Senate Republicans.

"Besides, we've known that Ted Cruz is a spineless slug for years, so there's not really a sense of urgency there. Plus, who wants to get close enough to Ted to shave his genitals for surgery? Nobody does," Snazback said, answering her own question. "Not even Heidi."

There is even growing support to impeach President Trump from the right. Prominent Republicans like Bill Kristol have been asking why Dems feel that the impeachment process is too risky politically.

APRIL 24, 2019

Pelosi Wishes 'the Founders Had Given Us Some Tool by Which to Hold a President Accountable'

WASHINGTON, D.C. — Speaker of the House Nancy Pelosi told reporters today that she is "dismayed, shocked, saddened, outraged, and very unhappy" with what she learned after reading the redacted Mueller Report.

Pelosi said reading the report made her want to "hold Trump accountable more than ever." She said that "so many Americans want him to be made to answer for his abuse of power." Speaker Pelosi said she's been stopped on the street a dozen times or more now and is told by various American citizens they want Donald Trump's power to be "checked and balanced against Congress's power."

However, she also doesn't "have the foggiest clue" how to do any of that.

"I just wish that there was some way, somehow, some mechanism that Congress had to do anything about it," Pelosi lamented. "If only the founders had given us some tool by which to hold a president accountable when you have evidence of his lawless disregard for the Constitution. But I can't think of anything like that at the moment, can you?"

A LITTLE BIT LOUDER AND A WHOLE LOT WORSE

Speaker Pelosi said that she and her staff are "poring over every legal document [they] can get their hands on." As of yet, though, she reports that they haven't been able to locate anything to help them in this situation. Pelosi says she knows that voters are looking to her for leadership, but that she is worried that she might not be able to find a way to "hold Trump's feet to the fire" by election time next year.

"What if I spend the next eighteen months or so painstakingly checking every document in the National Archives and I still can't find a way for us to hold Trump accountable," Pelosi asked the reporters. "I'll feel so devastated helpless. It's so strange. You'd think that somewhere maybe even in the Constitution there'd be a way for us to get rid of a guy who anyone with a pulse and an honest thought in their brains can see isn't fit for office. But, well, if it's out there, we haven't found it yet."

An aide brought Ms. Pelosi a glass of iced tea.

"Mmm. Peach mint," Pelosi said, prompting reporters to lean in and start scribbling notes furiously, "I just love peach mint tea, don't you? The combination of peach and mint is just fantastic!"

The reporters pulled back again, putting their pens away.

"I'm afraid that as completely damning as Mueller's report is, and as clearly as he handed the ball to us to hold the president to account," Pelosi said, "We're going to have to just wait for eighteen months and trust that somewhere along the line he'll start holding himself accountable. It's bound to happen eventually. Right? Right? Right guys?"

The White House did not respond to requests for comment.

APRIL 29, 2019

Trump to Give Robert E. Lee Posthumous Medal of Freedom

WASHINGTON, D.C. — Hours after heaping praise on Confederate General Robert E. Lee, President Donald Trump said he'd be issuing a posthumous Presidential Medal of Freedom to Lee.

Mr. Trump was put in the position to praise Lee because when former Vice-President Joe Biden entered the 2020 presidential raise officially yesterday, his kickoff video directly mentioned Trump's comments about a racist rally in Charlottesville in 2017. The rally was held by a known right-wing, white nationalist group called "Unite the Right," and after a day of angry, violent protest between the rally-goers and counter-protesters left one woman dead, run over by white supremacist that has since been convicted of her murder, Trump made one of his most famous statements of his presidency.

Holding a press conference in the wake of Charlottesville, Trump seemed to make an attempt to shield some of the white nationalists from blame, saying they were only there to protest a statue of Lee being taken down.

But you also had people that were very fine people on both

A LITTLE BIT LOUDER AND A WHOLE LOT WORSE

> *sides. You had people in that group – excuse me, excuse me. I saw the same pictures as you did. You had people in that group that were there to protest the taking down, of to them, a very, very important statue and the renaming of a park from Robert E. Lee to another name. (Politico)*

Biden's campaign announcement drew out the president, and he defended his 2017 comments, claiming that Lee, who fought for the cause of the Confederacy, which was literally an anti-American insurgency, was a "great general, whether you like it or not."

> *Trump told reporters outside the White House on Friday that Robert E. Lee was "a great general, whether you like it or not," continuing his praise for a Confederate figure whose statue was at the heart of the 2017 white supremacist rally in Charlottesville, Virginia. (Axios)*

President Trump decided a few hours later he wanted to further honor Lee.

"You know, it's time for the Party of Lincoln to give thanks to this great general," Trump said. "Because do we really think people would think so highly of Lincoln if he didn't have such a great general like Lee to fight against?"

Trump compared the relationship between Lincoln and Lee to that of pro-wrestlers.

APRIL

"Lincoln was a good guy, okay? I get it. I might not agree with him releasing all the southerner's urbans, but hey, I get it," Trump said, "He was the good guy. But every fan of wrestling knows the good guy ain't nothin' without a good heel. And Lee was prolly the best heel of them all!"

Trump says that initially, he wanted to do more than just honor Lee.

"I wanted to know if our Pentagon science nerds could just bring Bob back to life somehow, but those cucks told me we don't even have cloning tech like that," Trump said with extreme exasperation. "So I went with this freedom medal thingy instead."

When reporters asked why Trump was giving a freedom award to someone who literally fought to keep black people not free, he laughed. Then Trump farted, which he blamed on Sarah Huckabee Sanders. Then, he explained that the answer was "simple math."

"Sure, he actually fought for the opposite of freedom for black people," Trump admitted, "but they were only three-fifths of a person back then anyway, so isn't this all just a lot of math no one cares about?"

MAY

MAY 6, 2019

Trump: "Bob Mueller Shouldn't Testify Because He'd Exonerate Me Way Too Much!"

WASHINGTON, D.C. — President Trump lashed out on Twitter over the weekend at the idea of FBI Special Counsel Robert Mueller testifying before a House committee later this month.

Word broke in the last few days that congressional Democrats were seeking to secure the testimony from Mr. Mueller on around May 15th. In a pair of tweets, Mr. Trump blasted the idea of Mueller testifying, saying that Dems are simply looking for a "redo" on Mueller's investigation, which could not establish a criminal conspiracy between the Trump campaign and Russia during the 2016 election, and ultimately led a long trail of evidence of Trump's guilt on obstruction of justice, despite not fully recommending an indictment, citing long-standing Department of Justice guidelines against charging a sitting president.

In the past, Trump had said that he didn't have any issue with Mueller testifying. Attorney General William Barr told the Senate Judiciary Committee he also didn't mind Mueller speaking to Congress. But Trump's tweets seem to portray a sudden about-face, leaving some on the Hill wondering if there's anything Barr and Trump are still trying

A LITTLE BIT LOUDER AND A WHOLE LOT WORSE

to keep from the American public. Both the attorney general and president insist that Mueller's report exonerates Trump, despite the fact that even the redacted version of it specifically says Mueller's team was unable to exonerate Trump, and only that a criminal conspiracy with Russia couldn't be proven to a legal standard.

The jockeying over what, exactly, the Mueller Report says could be made moot by testimony from Mueller. There are many speculating that is the precise reason why his testimony is now something Trump doesn't want out in public view. This morning, House Democrats took their first steps toward holding Barr in contempt of Congress for not providing the unredacted Mueller Report along with the underlying evidence, as they had subpoenaed for last week.

On his way out of the Oval Office for a lunch break, Trump was stopped by the press pool on the White House lawn. The president was asked by reporters why he's not in favor of Mueller testifying any longer. Trump explained that he doesn't want people to "get the wrong idea."

"I mean, don't get me wrong, Mueller's Angry Democrat Witch Hunt Hoax Coup totally exonerated me," Trump explained. "But I'm afraid if he testifies, he'll say stuff that makes me sound too innocent, know what I mean? Bob Mueller shouldn't testify because he'd exonerate me way too much!"

Trump said that the same reason he doesn't want the unredacted Mueller Report released is the same reason he doesn't want Mueller testifying.

MAY

"My personal attorney general already told everyone all the good stuff. NO COLLUSION. NO OBSTRUCTION," Trump said. "If Mueller goes and tells Congress what he found in his own words, he could just end up drowning out Bill Barr, and making it seem that I'm, like way, way, way too innocent, know what I mean? Of course, you do. I don't even know what I mean, but you guys do."

MAY 8, 2019

Trump Promises: "We're Only Covering-Up How Innocent I Really, Truly Am, I Pinky Swear!"

WASHINGTON, D.C. — There is a battle currently going on between one-half of the legislative branch of government and Donald Trump's executive branch.

There is no denying that one very palpable and easily seen after effect of the 2018 midterm elections is that the Democratic Party is now the majority in the House of Representatives. For the first two years of presidency, Trump's party was in charge of both congressional chambers, and Democrats were often frustrated and angry at what they perceived as a lack of oversight being conducted on the administration. The Dems stormed into the majority last fall partly on the promise made by many candidates during the mid-terms to do exactly that, and employ the "checks and balances" that the country's government is supposed to operate on.

Since taking control of the House in January, the House committees on finance, judiciary, and intelligence have all issued various subpoenas for documents related to the first two years of the Trump Era. Ranging from an unredacted copy of the Mueller Report and its underlying evidence to the president's tax returns, House Dems

MAY

have been pushing as hard as they can for information they say they're legally entitled to.

Initially, President Trump said he had no problems with either FBI Special Counsel Robert Mueller or his former White House counsel Don McGahn testifying before the House committees. However, in the days and weeks, since the redacted Mueller report was delivered by Attorney General William Barr, accompanied by a 4-page summary that has been roundly criticized by both Democrats and some Republicans, tensions have risen between Trump and Congress, and his administration instructed McGahn not to comply with Democratic subpoenas, and the president has said he doesn't want Mueller to testify any longer.

Even some on the right are starting to smell a cover-up.

Today, Mr. Trump was spotted heading out to lunch and stopped on the front lawn of the White House. He was asked about whether he thought it might appear that he and his administration are hiding things and participating in a "cover-up." Trump laughed so hard at the suggestion that some gas escaped his colon, and he blamed that gas leak on Sarah Huckabee Sanders, his press secretary, but she was back inside the White House.

"Of course we're doing a cover-up! The best kind of cover-up! My cover-ups are always the best, of course, but this one is really big folks," Trump admitted. "But we're only covering up how innocent I really, truly am. I pinky swear!"

Trump says the American people "literally have no choice but to

A LITTLE BIT LOUDER AND A WHOLE LOT WORSE

believe" him.

"Seriously, try not believing me and see how fast my army men show up at your door to take you to one of Obama's FEMA camps that we actually built to put brown babies we kidnap in," Trump said. "But also, would a guy who lied to you more than 10,000 times in two years lie to you about this?"

No one answered Trump. It was very awkwardly silent for a least a solid minute. Trump just stared at each reporter, waiting for a response, but they were all too shocked by what they heard to respond.

"That's what I thought. Checkmate, libs, checkmate," Trump said, farting again.

This story is developing.

MAY 8, 2019

Gym Jordan: "Sure Trump Broke the Law, but What Right Do the American People Have to Know the Details?"

WASHINGTON, D.C. — Today, the House Judiciary Committee held a hearing on whether or not to send a resolution holding Attorney General William Barr in contempt of Congress.

At issue, Democrats believe Barr has been stonewalling efforts to get the unredacted Mueller Report and its underlying evidence from the Department of Justice. The hearing comes days after Barr pulled out of testimony before the same committee last week, citing the fact that Democrats wanted to have an outside counsel question him. However, Democrats pointed out that Supreme Court Justice Brett Kavanaugh's accuser was questioned by outside counsel during his confirmation hearing. Just before the hearing began, President Trump claimed executive privilege over the Mueller Report.

One of Barr's most vociferous defenders was Congressman Gym Jordan of Ohio. Jordan, a Republican, and several of his Republican colleagues spent the majority of the hearing railing against the idea of holding Barr in contempt. Jordan insisted that Democrats are wanting to "destroy" Barr and his credibility because he believes they are afraid of what Barr will uncover while he investigates the origins of the Mueller

A LITTLE BIT LOUDER AND A WHOLE LOT WORSE

investigation. Some on the Hill have started to question whether Jordan feels more loyalty to Trump and his political party than he does the country and its Constitution.

Moments ago, our reporter caught up Gym Jordan and asked him about the hearing. Jordan said he is "100% on the side of the American people," but "really only the ones who love Trump with all their hearts." Jordan admitted that the actual contents of the Mueller Report "certainly show several places where Trump broke the law," but Jordan defended Trump's actions, saying he was "super-duper sad and upset about being investigated." Beyond Trump's state of mind and emotional state, however, Jordan says there's a larger reason he doesn't want House Democrats, or the American public, to see the unredacted report or its supporting evidence.

"The bottom line for me is really very simple," Jordan told our reporter, "Sure, Trump broke the law, but what right do the American people have to know the details?"

An obviously flustered, and possibly coked-up Jordan, continued.

"I mean, seriously, what do this liberal whackaloon crazy Democrats think this is, a free society where people have a right to know if their president is a manifestly lawless, self-evidently corrupt person who abuses his authority with reckless disregard for the rule of law," Jordan demanded. "I'm sorry, but the Constitution doesn't give you the right to hold your president accountable. It gives that right to Congress, and I'm a Congress! I'm a Congress! I AM A CONGRESS! SO THEREFORE IF I DON'T WANNA, I DON'T GOTTA!"

MAY

Jordan, really upset, just kept ongoing.

"Yes, of course, the Mueller Report makes it clear that Trump has and will continue to break the law whenever he wants to, but who cares? Seriously, who cares? I asked all my friends and family and they don't care. So what makes you uppity libs think you have a right to know how exactly he broke the law? And what's the point? We Republicans aren't even going to admit that we see the plain truth in front of us, even though you're rubbing our noses in it like so many Russian women."

"I'm frankly really upset at the idea that anyone would even want to see the Mueller Report after we've spent so much time telling you what you should think is in it," Jordan insisted. "Trump isn't Hillary Clinton. He doesn't deserve to have his actions called into question! He's a Republican, and therefore, I'm pretty sure the Constitution says pretty clear he's not subject to checks or balances!"

No one could stop Jordan if they wanted to.

"Sure, no one is above the law, I get that. In theory, I believe that but I mean, you know, REPUBLICAN PARTY, TAXES ARE THEFT," Jordan was shouting, "OBAMA HATES GUNS! OH SHIT! I ALMOST FORGOT, AND THIS WILL BE MY FINAL WORD ON ALL OF THIS NONSENSE: BENGHAZI!"

Gym Jordan snapped his fingers and disappeared in a cloud of smoke and ignored charges of sexual misconduct.

MAY 9, 2019

Hillary to Trump Jr.: "Oh, You Already Testified Before Congress? I Can Benghazi How Difficult That Might Be"

WASHINGTON, D.C. — In a rather unforeseen nexus of events, former Secretary of State Hillary Rodham Clinton just happened to run into First Son Donald Trump Jr. at a D.C. area pie shop, and reportedly, the two exchanged brief, but terse words with one another.

Last night, news broke the Senate Intelligence Committee had issued a new subpoena to the president's third smartest son in relation to contacts he had with Russia during the 2016 presidential election. Trump Jr. was at the center of one of the key incidents reported on by FBI Special Counsel Robert Mueller because he met with Russian attorneys at Trump Tower during the summer of that year. The president publicly admitted to helping his son draft a completely false and misleading letter about the meeting, claiming it was about American adoption law, when in reality the younger Trump would later admit that he took the meeting, which was also attended by Trump's son-in-law Jared Kushner and now jailed former campaign manager Paul Manafort, to get "dirt" that was offered to him on Ms. Clinton.

"Ah, Junior, funny running into you here at the pie shop," Secretary Clinton was overheard telling Mr. Trump Jr., "Hey, thoughts

MAY

and prayers little guy on that whole congressional testimony thing. But I think you'll do just fine. You really only get in trouble if you lie to Congress, but you're definitely smart enough to not do that. Oh wait, I kinda remember that being all over the Mueller Report. My bad."

Donald Trump Jr. reportedly told Clinton he'd already testified before, and he didn't think it was fair that he'd have to do it again. That line of defense has been trotted out by Trump loyalists all over social media. The moment word broke that the committee, which is led by a member of Trump's own party, had issued the subpoena, tweets started being sent defending Trump Jr. because he'd already testified before.

Congressman Gym Jordan took time away from his work inserting the president all the way down his throat, past his esophagus, and into his tummy to tweet support for Donald Trump Jr.

Senator Chuck Grassley even stopped literally fucking a dinosaur fossil he used to date back in his day and had supportive comments for the president's son.

"Oh," Secretary Clinton was heard telling Trump Jr. back at the pie shop, "Did you already testify before congress? I can Benghazi how difficult that might be."

With sarcasm so thick it could be detected by the EPA administration just a few blocks away, Clinton continued to mock the man whose own father probably will call him "fake news" within a few days.

"Yeah, I mean. Gosh, Don Jr., It must be really hard to have to talk about the same exact thing over and over again, no matter what

A LITTLE BIT LOUDER AND A WHOLE LOT WORSE

investigations clear your name," Clinton said. "Oh wait, sorry. I forgot that Mueller didn't exonerate you, he just said you're too dumb to prosecute."

Before heading into the pie shop to eat her pie, Ms. Clinton gave the younger Trump some advice for testifying before a Senate committee for the second time.

"First, and I know this is going to be really hard for you Junior, so don't give yourself too much grief if you can't do it," Clinton began, "but, try not to lie. At least, don't lie so much. That's it, really. Just, don't lie to Congress under oath. You know, if you can help it."

A stunned Donald Jr. watched Clinton turn on her heel and walk away. Then, she quickly turned back, startling him as she yelled.

"LOCK HIM UP!," Clinton screamed, cackling. "Hey, wait right there, Junior, and I'll bring you some humble pie."

This is a developing story.

MAY 23, 2019

Mitch McConnell: "Trump's Not Above the Law, It Just Doesn't Apply to Him"

WASHINGTON, D.C. — Senate Majority Leader Mitch McConnell told reporters outside the rotunda today that he's "sick and tired of the Democrats treating President Trump like he's President Obama." McConnell said that "obstructing Democrat presidents is the solemn duty of every red-blooded patriotic American." However, Leader McConnell blasted the investigations currently underway by House Democrats, calling them "dangerous checks and balances" and "wanton accountability."

"I get a distinct impression that my friends across the aisle think that I think President Trump is above the law, and that's just so wrongheaded I cannot begin to tell you," McConnell explained. "Sure, he's denying the Democrats oversight into his administration that I would literally be foaming at the mouth to impeach the previous black administration over, but I don't think that. No one's above the law."

Pausing to sniff some coal he had in his pants pocket, McConnell saw the reporters were confused.

"Trump's not above the law," McConnell posited, "it just doesn't apply to him."

A LITTLE BIT LOUDER AND A WHOLE LOT WORSE

McConnell explained his rationale further.

"It might look like I'm saying President Trump is above the law. I get that. But let me just reiterate — I do not think Trump is above the law," McConnell said emphatically. "I just think the law is irrelevant to him."

The Kentucky Republican, sensing perhaps that his point was still not quite being made clearly, continued.

"What I'm getting at is this — the law isn't important to Trump," McConnell said. "No? Still not buying it? Okay, um, oh! Let's try this! So, Trump is NOT above the law, at all, okay? The law just can't be used to hold him accountable. That makes sense right?"

Reporters were scratching their heads.

"Man! You guys are tough today," McConnell said with exasperation in his voice. "But I'll get you there. I'll get you to understand."

Leader McConnell removed a hunk of coal from his coat pocket. He put the coal down his pants and started rubbing it on his crotch. McConnell explained that's how he does his best thinking.

"Ah! I got it! Ready? This one will really make it all crystal clear to you folks, I'm sure of it," McConnell said, a smile creeping across his face. "It's not that I think President Trump is above the law, it's just that I think it shouldn't impact him in any way."

Trump did a "Ta-da!" move with his hands, expecting applause. When he was met with more silence, he sighed heavily. McConnell rubbed his chin for a moment, black coal ash smearing across his face.

MAY

"Alright, I'm gonna try this one more time, you hear me? And then we gotta wrap this up because if I don't have the blood of innocent brown babies pumped into my tortoise veins every two hours, I die," McConnell said. "It's part of the deal I made with Satan to stay in power. Anyhow, here's how I see it: President Trump is not above the law; the is just beneath the office of the presidency. Get it? Got it? Good."

Reached for comment, Speaker of the House Nancy Pelosi (D-CA) said she's "so upset" by what McConnell said that she'd "very strongly consider maybe possibly one day perhaps perchance doing something about it."

"But I'm not sure yet," Pelosi said. "I have to get the polling data back to see if the Constitution is worth enough to the voters for us to defend. Just trust that I know more than you, okay? I'm playing, like 1,398th-dimensional chess here, okay? Trump will either rein himself in, or we'll maybe perhaps probably I hope to beat him next year after we spend this year not inspiring our base with the political courage to impeach a lawless president. Make sense? Of course, it does! I'm Nancy Pelosi!"

This story is developing.

MAY 24, 2019

Donald Trump Jr.'s Book on Hold While Doctors Fish the Crayon out of His Nose

NEW YORK, NEW YORK — The Second Smartest Donald Trump in the World, son of the President of the United States, has inked a book deal, according to several reports. President Donald Trump's third most intelligent son, Donald Trump Jr., has announced a deal with publisher Center Street Press. The financial details of the book were not disclosed. There is not a title for the new book, either. However, Mr. Trump Jr. says he will address the "great achievements" of his father's presidential administration in it.

Though the book deal is quite fresh, word out of Trump Land is that Junior already had to put the book on hold for emergency medical reasons. A team of doctors is currently trying to remove the crayon he was using to write his tome from Trump Jr.'s left nostril. There was already a Lego piece in his right nostril, further complicating the issue.

"Just after noon, our switchboard received an urgent call from Donald Trump Jr.'s executive assistant, stating that he'd gotten a crayon lodged up inside his nose and that everyone was afraid he'd pull his brain cell out with it if he tried too hard," Dr. Kenneth Kilroy of St. Mary's Hospital of the Upper West Side told reporters just moments

MAY

ago. "Within moments we had an ambulance en route and the best pediatricians on our staff were in it, headed for Mr. Trump Jr.'s office."

Upon arriving, doctors found a frantic Donald Trump Jr...

"GET IT OUT! GET IT OUT! MOMMY! GET IT OUT," Trump Jr. was heard screaming. "I got da crown stuck in my nose, MOMMY!"

The medical staff was alarmed to find the crayon, small and orange, lodged extremely tightly in the president's son's nose. The junior Trump kept flailing around and crying as doctors tried to calm him down enough to attempt an extraction of the crayon. Nothing they did seemed to work though.

"GET THE CROWN OUT! IT'S HURTING MY BRAIN, MOMMY," Trump Jr. howled.

It's unclear at this time how long it will take the team to remove the crayon. Even though both nostrils are blocked, doctors are convinced Trump Jr. won't have any problems inhaling or exhaling.

"Normally we'd be worried about both nostrils plugged, but he's been a mouth-breather his whole life, so he'll be just fine," Dr. Kilroy said.

The White House is said to have been alerted to the situation, but since it doesn't involve his daughter Ivanka or his other daughter, The Not Ivanka Blonde one, the president doesn't care.

JUNE

JUNE 3, 2019

After 14 Hours in the UK Without Fox News, President Convinced Donald Trump Is Danger to America

LONDONTOWNSHIPSHIRE, ENGLANDVILLE KINGDOM — Upon arriving in the United Kingdom for a three-day state visit, one of the first things the President of the United States did was take note of the fact that his state media outlets are not easily found on UK airwaves. The president tweeted his displeasure about the situation this morning.

The most powerful man in the world even seemed to initiate a boycott of CNN's parent company via Twitter.

Reportedly, the president has spent much of his time while not being given tours by Queen Elizabeth and Prince Charles seeking out some Fox News programming. According to several sources close enough to him to get a good whiff of the Borscht and piss cologne he got as a gift from Russian President Vlad Putin, the commander in chief has been forced to get updates on American news from CNN, and after 14 hours without Fox News to counteract it, something quite unexpected has happened. The president now believes that Donald Trump is a threat to America.

"Wow! Why didn't anyone tell me this Donald Trump guy was out there attacking our constitutional freedoms and giving aid and comfort

A LITTLE BIT LOUDER AND A WHOLE LOT WORSE

to white supremacists before," the president apparently asked Press Secretary Sarah Huckabee Sanders this evening at dinner. "I saw on CNN that he's told like over 10,000 lies since he was sworn in, and apparently the Mueller Report illustrates a specific pattern of abuse of his powers and specific instances where he clearly obstructed justice."

The president believes Trump represents a "bigly danger to the safety and prosperity of the United States."

"His tariff wars are turning farmers into welfare kings. His rhetoric is getting bombs sent to his political adversaries," the president said, "and his entire administration is willfully ignoring constitutional oversight. Hell, that's the exact stuff that Nixon was nearly impeached for! It seems to me like the United States can't afford to just sit back and let Trump keep doing this, which makes me wonder why Nancy Pelosi hasn't been more vocal about considering impeachment."

The president said he was "outraged and alarmed" by what he heard on CNN about Donald Trump. Apparently, he was "blown away" by the fact that Fox News never told him any of these things about Trump.

"Why didn't Fox News tell me the idiot doesn't get how tariffs only make things more expensive for American consumers? Why didn't Fox tell me he has years worth of questionable ties to Russian oligarchs," the president asked incredulously. "I'm starting to get the sneaking and sinking feeling that Fox News hasn't been entirely truthful about this Donald Trump fellow, and that could pose a real, serious problem for all of us."

JUNE

When he arrives back in the United States, the president plans to convene a meeting of his most trusted advisers to determine how best to handle the "Donald Trump situation."

"I want to hear from the President of Puerto Rico, the President of Idaho, John Barron, and David Dennison," the president reportedly told Huckabee Sanders today. "When I get back, convene a meeting for me and them in the Executive Time suite, Sarah."

Huckabee had a question for her boss.

"You mean your bathroom toilet, right sir," Huckabee asked.

The president patted her on her head.

"Yes! That's a good Sarah! You got it right! So very good Sarah! Here," the president said, handing her a treat, "have a treat my good girl! Who's a good girl? That's right, Sarah! You are!"

Reportedly, Ms. Huckabee Sanders is desperate to make sure her brother knows she's not really a dog, even though the president treats her like one.

JUNE 6, 2019

Steven Crowder Hates Socialism so Much He Thinks Trump Should Nationalize YouTube and Force Them to Monetize Him

MIERDA EN LA CABEZA, TEXAS — Scientists aren't quite sure what right-wing YouTube star Steven Crowder is. He claims to be a "comedian," but there hasn't been anything he's said or done that can be peer-reviewed as "comedy." However, given that this is still, for now, a relatively free country, Crowder is not required by law to be completely truthful, and therefore, he claims that he is, in fact, a comedian.

Now, though, he's a comedian who has lost access to YouTube's monetization features because of his attacks on Vox journalist Carlos Maza. Crowder has tried rallying his forces and getting fellow conservatives riled up about losing ad revenue from YouTube under the hashtag "#VoxAdpocalypse." Even Senator Ted Cruz (R-TX) has taken time away from his busy schedule of using the zodiac to be instructed on who to murder next and weighed in on Crowder's punishment for calling Maza, among other things, a "lispy fag" and using "Mexican" in the pejorative sense about him.

Crowder spends much of his "broadcast" time bashing socialism, who he thinks is a socialist, and generally, anything he considers to be derived from or about socialism. Though the First Amendment of the

JUNE

Constitution of the United States does guarantee a right to free speech, the judicial system has largely allowed private companies to dictate what content they will host and provide the public access to. For example, the government cannot tell *The Washington Post* to run a story claiming Donald Trump is the literal son of God. Crowder told his YouTube audience today, however, that he thinks the government "absolutely should be able to force YouTube" to host his content and pay him for it.

"Don't you all see? Socialism is so bad that we simply have to fight it with every weapon we have, even if that means nationalizing YouTube," Crowder yelled into the camera last night. "Sometimes you have to use the force of the government to defend free-market capitalist values, fam."

Mr. Crowder believes that even though he can't find it specifically written it, "capitalism is directly enshrined in the Constitution." As such, he believes the government has the right and duty to "strip private companies of their autonomy" and force them to run any content the government desires.

"Communism and socialism are so evil that we have to be willing to put the boot of the government down on the necks of any company who doesn't want to pay me money for calling people fags," Crowder insisted. "If we are not willing as a country to tell a private company they have to pay me money for making 90's era jokes about someone's sexuality, what exactly are we willing to defend?"

Crowder is scheduled to have a sit-down meeting with White

A LITTLE BIT LOUDER AND A WHOLE LOT WORSE

House Senior genocide and racism adviser Stephen Miller next week to discuss their options.

"We're both smarmy, smug assholes with basically the same name," Crowder said, "so I think this will go really well. Plus, I'm white and conservative so I'm pretty sure that means Miller's gonna be on my side no matter what I propose."

This is a developing story.

JUNE 10, 2019

Trump Economic Adviser: Eliminating Minimum Wage Will Result in 0% Unemployment

WASHINGTON, D.C. — The man who will potentially take over for outgoing White House economic adviser Kevin Hassett told reporters today that the Trump administration has a radical new approach to the minimum wage that they'd like to see in the next federal budget.

Tom Thompaulsen, a Republican elected state representative who is no stranger to the media, says that he hopes to have Hassett's job in a few weeks and that his new budget proposal should be a "rallying cry" for fiscal conservatives. Thompaulsen says his budget will do "exactly what Republicans want budgets to do" which is to slash taxes on the top tiers and privatize social programs. However, Thompaulsen says that he intends to add one more gift to the American right-wing in the new budget — killing the minimum wage altogether.

"I ask you this," began Thompaulsen at a recent press conference in front of Knavery Financial — an investment brokerage company run by Charles Knavery, heir to the Knavery Capital empire — "What good ever comes of government trying to help anything? The government can't do anything right. The government is terrible at everything it does. The minimum wage is no different, and that's why it's time for it to go."

A LITTLE BIT LOUDER AND A WHOLE LOT WORSE

His staffers say that Thompaulsen is not completely set on adding language to strip the Fair Labor Standards Act of 1938 of its establishment of a minimum wage, but that he is definitely leaning that direction.

"When the FLSA was passed, the minimum wage was twenty-five cents an hour. Maybe if it stayed at that rate," Thompaulsen said, "I'd be singing another tune. After all, I think two-bits for an hour's worth of hard work is a fair deal, but the fact is this out of control government spending has raised that rate to a whopping $7.25 an hour! What business can afford to pay its employees at that rate? That's an increase of more than 28 times over eighty years!"

"Government spending is evil," Rep. Thompaulsen said as he adjusted the tie he paid for out of his taxpayer salary, "There's nothing worse than government spending, but government picking winners and losers by choosing who gets paid what wage? That's a pretty darned close second if you ask me."

Thompaulsen says there's a major economic reason to lower the minimum wage to zero as well.

"The simple fact is, and fiscal conservatives have been saying this since 1938, that a minimum wage suppresses employment, " Mr. Thompaulsen said, continuing, "We know for a fact that raising the minimum wage causes a rise in unemployment. Of course, by 'fact' we mean 'after cherry-picking all the studies that show us the conclusion we want.' So if we reduce the minimum wage to zero dollars and zero cents an hour, we should see 0% unemployment!"

JUNE

"We could have stopped the Great Recession in its tracks," Thompaulsen claimed, "if we had told those three-quarters of a million people losing their jobs each month that they could get right back in the workforce if they'd accept sharecroppers' wages! We need to take down the barriers between allowing someone to volunteer for slavery and the Federal government."

A reporter from *The Ft. Georgia Observer* asked Thompaulsen if having no minimum wage ensured full employment, why the Great Depression wasn't over on October 30th, 1929 when everyone who lost their jobs could just go and work for free.

Thompaulsen blinked twice.

"Oh I see, you went to a liberal indoctrination college," Rep. Thompaulsen surmised, "I bet you think Calvin Coolidge was a bad president huh? Well, I'll remind you that FDR built internment camps for the Japanese and other bad stuff too, so, um. Benghazi that, dude. Benghazi that."

JUNE 12, 2019

Texas Business Has Been Making Millions on Its "Lunch With Ted Cruz" Escape Room

EL CHINGADERO, TEXAS — All across America, "escape room" businesses have been cropping up.

In general, an escape room is a business that offers customers the chance to be locked inside a room and given a time limit under which they must find clues that allow them to exit. One such business in a small Texas town announced yesterday that one of the new themed rooms they've opened up has been "raking in millions of dollars" since they made it available to the public a couple of weeks ago.

"A couple of weeks ago, Ted Cruz sent out a mailer to people offering to give donors a lunch date with him," Candace Snoot, owner of Breakout Rooms in El Chingadero, told us today via Skype. "And that made us realize there are probably millions of people, not just in Texas, but around the country, that would pay money to get as far the hell away from Ted as possible, and so the Lunch Date with Ted Cruz escape experience was born."

Of course, Senator Cruz has a busy schedule of copying the Bible into the Constitution and making long-winded, grandstanding speeches during Senate hearings, so he cannot be present in the escape room. But

JUNE

Ms. Snoot says she and her family came up with a solution for an analog for Cruz.

"We take a giant burlap sack full of slugs and put a Bluetooth speaker in it that blasts Breitbart headlines and Bible verses," Snoot said. "People so far have said they feel like they were in the same room with Senator Cruz."

Snoot told us that the success of the Cruz room was almost instantaneous, but not at all surprising to her.

"How many more repugnant people are there out there in the world? I think, maybe one or two, tops," Snoot said. "We weren't sure if people would want to pay money for doing what their natural survival instincts would do, but I suspect we'd have similar success with an Escape from Rectal Cancer Room, for example."

Snoot says they also play on Cruz's earlier career to create an "aura of fright and dismay" in the room.

"We put zodiac signs all over the room, reminding you all the time that Ted is, of course, the Zodiac Killer," Snoot said. "People say this is the scariest escape room we've ever made."

While trying to follow the clues to get away from the fake Ted Cruz in the room with them, customers must try to find a way to ignore the rhetoric blasting out of the Bluetooth speaker. Snoot says she spent days going over C-SPAN clips of the scariest Cruz soundbites she could find. Snoot doesn't think customers are ever disappointed with what she used.

"You try listening to a syllable come out of his mouth without being absolutely terrified," Snoot said. "The best part is that even if you aren't terrified by what you hear, there's always a good chance that he'll literally bore you to death, and in our industry, that's a big, big, big plus."

Candace says her business has never been better. People have booked the Cruz room so far out that she's considering adding other, similar experiences. If business keeps up, she may have to find a bigger building, too.

"Oh man, there are so many options! We could have dinner with Stephen Miller, or we could use Texas' own Louie Gohmert, that man is so stupid he makes wet mud look like a Rhodes Scholar," Candace said. "But we're not sure that escaping from someone just because they're dumb is enough, so we'll make sure to get all of Gohmert's racist stupidity to play out of the speaker."

Sen. Cruz's office could not be reached for comment.

JUNE 25, 2019

Local Conservative Outraged at Liberal's 'Vulgar Display of Empathy and Compassion'

COLD CAVE HILLS, TENNESSEE — Jethro Bohiggins is "sick and fucking tired" of seeing liberals and progressives in his small Tennessee town feed the homeless. The right-wing podcaster and singer/songwriter told his audience today that when he sees a liberal in his town telling someone they should be able to use any bathroom that makes them feel comfortable, regardless of their genitals at birth, he wants to "shit a purple Twinkie."

"I can't be the only one who has had it up to here with all this caring and stuff," Bohiggins ranted, "because we all know 'caring' is just a liberal elitist word for 'government control.' I'm sorry, fam, but I ain't gonna let no goddamn government tell me I can't judge people based on the color of their skin without being called an insensitive, racist jerk for it!"

Bohiggins says "America is rotten from within" because "good, clean, moral, upstanding, God-fearing, gun-toting, ammo hoarding American patriots" feel like they can't exercise their freedom of speech freely.

"What good is free speech if it has consequences, anyway, fam? I ask you this," Jethro said, "in all earnest sincerity. Isn't the whole point of free speech to be an obtuse, ignorant douchebag and never be called an obtuse, ignorant douchebag for what you say? I sure think so, and my barely ninth-grade civics understanding says that's true, so it clearly must be!"

Jethro then recounted the events of an encounter he had with a longtime friend over the weekend. The two were out to eat at a local barbecue establishment when they were approached by a homeless man. Without hesitating, Bohiggins' friend gave the homeless veteran a five-dollar bill. Jethro saw a teaching moment and gave the homeless veteran a lesson in personal economic responsibility.

"Now, if giving the homeless guy free money wasn't bad enough, let me tell you, something," Jethro told his audience. "I and Jerry got into a heated argument at the table because I said I thought that it'd be better if we just built a big catapult and launched the migrant babies we kidnap back over the border, instead of spending good American money keeping semi-Mexican-ish people dirty and malnourished."

Jerry apparently told Jethro he thought the catapult was "mean and heartless" and said that in America, it seems ridiculous and insulting to tell small babies we're too full and too poor to help.

"Can you believe that vulgar display of empathy and compassion, fam? I tell you what, as soon as I picked my jaw up off the floor, I hit Jerry with the most logically concise, brilliant conservative argument I could," Jethro explained, "and I don't think he'd ever been called a 'Libtard' out loud like that before, so I won that argument hands-fuckin'-

JUNE

down, y'all."

For Bohiggins, whether or not to be compassionate or empathetic comes down to a "very simple question."

"Where does it say I have to be compassionate in the Constitution? Where does it say in the Constitution I have to care about others," Jethro asked rhetorically. "Sure that stuff is in the Bible, but if you think a Christian actually uses the Bible as their guidelines for behavior, I have a Mueller Report that exonerates the president to sell you."

JUNE 27, 2019

DNC Informs Registered Dems Who They Should Think Won First Debates

WASHINGTON, D.C. — The Democratic Party is holding its first two primary debates of the 2020 presidential election season. In previous years, there wouldn't have been likely been a need to split the debates up over more than one night, but with over 456 declared candidates, sources say the DNC was given very little choice but to do just that. Last night, several candidates, including emerging favorite Sen. Elizabeth Warren of Massachusetts squared off on MSNBC, and tonight another round of candidates including former Vice President Joe Biden will take the stage.

Though the second debate has yet to take place, the Democrats reportedly wanted to "get out in front" of any speculation and declare a winner. Normally, it might not be common practice for a political party to dictate to its voters who they should think won a debate, but one very highly placed source told us on the condition of anonymity that Democratic leadership doesn't "want a repeat of 2016."

"We were way too subtle. Too many superdelegates. We don't think it was quite obvious enough who we were telling everyone to vote for," our source said, "because, you know, it was her turn. We will never

JUNE

understand for the life of us why, 'Just because it's her turn now' wasn't a more compelling campaign slogan, but here we are anyway."

To completely eliminate any doubt as to who the DNC wants its voters to support as early as possible, an email and text alert was sent to every registered Democrat. The messages thanked everyone for their continued "continued loyalty to the party" and then stated in bold, all-caps letters, who the debate winner was, even though voters are still waiting to see the second round of debates.

"They don't need to see another debate to know who won them both," our source said. "Let's not go having a real primary season where we really and truly vet candidates to figure out if they're the right one to lead the country. That seems, frankly, like a lot of work that none of us have time for anymore. It's just really a great time-saving thing to have all your opinions dictated to you, isn't it?"

Our source said that rank and file voters should not be "alarmed or offended" by the party trying to force another candidate on them.

"Thinking is hard, and deciding is even harder, and we think our voters appreciate not having to do either," our source proclaimed. "And if anyone thinks they know what their voters want more than the voters themselves, it's we, Democrats."

Apparently, the DNC considered doing the same thing in 2016 but reconsidered.

"Frankly we were still trying to figure out just how far we could cram her down everyone's throats, which was odd considering she was on track to do just fine in the popular vote, and she did," our source

A LITTLE BIT LOUDER AND A WHOLE LOT WORSE

said. "Someone the other day asked us what would have happened if she had campaigned a little harder in the Rust Belt instead of us smugly assuming she'd win those states easily, and of course I did what any sensible person would do — I jumped out of the window so I didn't have to ponder that hypothetical since it hurts my brain to do so."

Registered Democrats should receive the email and text messages by the middle of the day.

JULY

JULY 1, 2019

Fox News Offers Time Slot Before Tucker Carlson to Kim Jong-Un

NEW YORK, NEW YORK — Executives at Fox News have reportedly reached out to North Korean Dictator Kim Jong-Un and offered him the time slot on their primetime lineup that is currently occupied by Martha MacCallum, which immediately precedes Tucker Carlson's show.

The development comes in the wake of President Donald Trump's historic visit to the demilitarized zone between North and South Korea this weekend. During the visit, Mr. Trump shook hands with and met Kim Jong-Un. The president had offered to meet with the North Korean dictator who is accused of murdering his own brother, among others, on Twitter after leaving the G20 summit in Japan.

Some pundits and commentators noticed that Fox News' coverage of the impromptu summit had a decidedly different tone than when rumors of former President Barack Obama's attempts to restart relations with North Korea broke. Even noted conservative voices, like former Congressman Joe Walsh, noted that Fox's hosts, who pilloried Kim Jong-Un for years as a barbaric autocrat, had begun to praise him, ignoring the multiple human rights violations he and his deceased father are accused of perpetrating on their own people.

A LITTLE BIT LOUDER AND A WHOLE LOT WORSE

"It is with great honor that we invite President Emperor King Donald J. Trump's most cherished and honored friend, North Korean Super Nice Guy Leader Kim Jong-Un to join the Fox News klan," a press release from Fox News reads. "We are certain that a very special, very legal, very cool bond has been formed between Dear President and the North Korean very warm and friendly leader, and look forward to leveraging that special bond for ratings."

It's unclear exactly which time slot would be given to Ms. MacCallum should the North Korean dictator take Fox News up on their offer. Fox News Jr. Media Executive Dan Dently told investors on a conference call this morning that was "not a very big concern for us."

"A man needs something, and a woman will have to give that something up. Sounds to me like the rock-ribbed Republican conservative values this station defends against the onslaught of a liberal slant toward facts we don't like to know," Dently said. "I'm sure we have SOME position for her. I mean…this is Fox News after all. O'Reilly might be gone and Ailes might be dead, but there's still enough weapons-grade misogyny in here to base six seasons of *Handmaid's Tale* on."

Tucker Carlson, the man who would be tasked with following the North Korean dictator's show, told reporters today he'd be "thrilled" for the chance.

"I already spend an hour every night kissing a wannabe autocrat's ass, I might as well kiss a real one's ass, too," Carlson said.

For his part, Kim Jong-Un has not given any solid indications one

JULY

way or the other about taking the Fox News job. He did, however, tell North Korean state media outlets that he's hired a television producer and has started to "think about the format" of his show. Reportedly, a late-night talk show is what is favored by Kim Jong-Un.

"Leader Kim has reached out to Dennis Rodman to see if he'd be his Andy Richter," one source close to the North Korean despot told reporters on the condition of anonymity. "He's pretty sure Mike Huckabee will be his bandleader, and his daughter Sarah will be head joke writer. Because, you know, she was always being so funny at her press conferences all the time."

JULY 5, 2019

Trump Blames 4th of July Rain on 'Bob Mueller's Team of Angry Democrats'

WASHINGTON, D.C. — Yesterday, President Donald Trump got his wish and the nation's capital played host to a military parade. Mr. Trump had been pushing for such an event since he attended Bastille Day celebrations in France shortly after becoming president. While it's unclear what the attendance for the parade would have been like on a perfectly sunny, clear day, it's quite possible that crowds were further discouraged from attending by the rain that fell on the parade.

President Trump tweeted yesterday that the weather shouldn't keep people from showing up, but this morning he lashed out angrily about the rain, which he said was "either a Fake News enemy of the people hoax" or "part of Bob Mueller's Team of Angry Democrats' attempted coop on my administration."

"They can't coop me! No one can coop me! Lots of people have tried to coop me, but I get out every time because I'm not a chicken," Trump shouted at reporters. "I am sure there were at least six million people at the parade yesterday. I personally counted, at least, three or four million myself and only stopped counting because I had to go give that speech. By the way, and I'm pretty sure you can believe this

JULY

because I pay people really good money to tell me things I like to hear, people are calling my 4th of July speech the most important, best speech ever given by any president…maybe the best speech ever given anyone for all of time."

President Trump believes that without FBI Special Counsel Robert Mueller's interference, the weather during yesterday's parade and festivities would have been "bigly sunny and mighty warm."

"He couldn't let me win though, could he? He couldn't pin any crimes on me, so he got his little do-over with all his eight trillion Angry Democrats," Trump railed, "and they made it rain. I don't know how they made it rain, but I have some mildly stupid theories, as well as a handful that are just outright racist. Like, are we sure that Colin Kaepernick didn't do some kind of uppity urban rain dance? Did Previous Black Administration put a Sharia hex on me at the request of Conflicted Bob Mueller? Congress should be investigating that, not the multitude of obvious crimes I've committed!"

Special Counsel Mueller is scheduled to testify before House committees on July 17th, and President Trump says that he wants Republicans on the committees to make sure they "grill" Mueller about his role in the Independence Day rain storms.

"Quite frankly if I don't see Louis Gohmert, Gym Jordan, and Mark Warner doing their best to grill Conflicted Bob Mueller about the rain," Trump shouted, "then I think they need to be, probably, shot. Executed. For treason. We're looking into that and a whole lot of other very cool, very legal things we can do. My Attorney General, you

A LITTLE BIT LOUDER AND A WHOLE LOT WORSE

know, my personal Attorney General Bill Barr? He says I can literally do whatever the fuck I want, whenever the fuck I want to. And why would he lie? When has Bill Barr ever known to be someone who will just unrepentantly lie, with a straight face, or maybe even a smug, self-satisfied shit-eating grin? That sound like Bill Barr to you? Of course, it doesn't!"

JULY 8, 2019

Fox News Hires David Dennison as New Programming Director

NEW YORK, NEW YORK — This morning, Fox News announced that it has hired presidential confidante David Dennison to be their new director of programming at the network. The hiring decision comes after a weekend of blistering, withering criticism from President Trump about Fox's weekend news and commentary team.

Mr. Trump used Twitter to bash away at Fox News, even though his base makes up a substantial portion of Fox News viewership. It's unclear at this time, but perhaps part of Trump's ire arose from the fact that a barroom chant of "Fuck Trump!" was broadcast from France after the U.S. women's soccer team won their second World Cup in a row. Trump had been sparring publicly with Megan Rapinoe, the team's star left-winger, and he is not what many would consider a very popular world leader outside the states.

"Obviously it took us all very much so by surprise when Trump went off on us as he did," one anonymous Fox News executive told us. "Because Sean had just taken the president out of his mouth not five minutes prior, and he said that Trump didn't give him any indications of being unhappy. He didn't complain that Sean was using too many teeth, or not enough teeth, or even that Sean doesn't let Donald call him Ivanka anymore. According to Hannity, the president was in fine spirits before he heard that barroom chant."

Execs knew that they had to do something, our source told us. Fox has an exclusive deal with the White House to be its official state-sponsored TV programming. Competition from other conservative news outlets like One America News Network and the Stormfront KKK pamphlets has made Fox News particularly keen on keeping Trump happy. That's why Hannity is available to Trump whenever his presidential wick needs lighting, and also why they decided to move quickly and install a new programming director.

Initially, Trump himself was at the top of the shortlist of candidates.

"Yeah, we thought about hiring Trump himself because he clearly doesn't spend all his time doing presidential stuff," our source admitted, "but we also weren't sure if that meant we'd have to file for Chapter 11 as soon as we brought him on, or if we'd have to wait for him to drive the network into the ground first."

So, they set their sights elsewhere.

"We knew we had to hire someone Trump likes. Someone he trusts," our source said. "Initially, he asked us to hire the President of Puerto Rico, but after looking into it, Puerto Rico's laws wouldn't allow it. So he suggested his old friend David Dennison, and after some brief contract negotiations, Mr. Dennison agreed to join the team. It was quite convenient for us that he just happened to be in the Oval Office

JULY

with the president when we called Trump to discuss new program directors."

Mr. Dennison's exact salary is not being divulged, however, our source tells us it's an amount sufficient enough for Dennison to have called it "bigly great." There will also be certain fringe benefits that Dennison is entitled to, as an employee of Fox News.

"Of course, he'll be offered the full complement of options in the Ailes Package," our source divulged. "Or he can go with the O'Reilly Package. Either way, he's going to get to play a lot of grab-ass with frightened interns and shocked career journalists, that's for sure. The president seemed really jealous of Dennison's deal, that's for sure."

For his part, President Trump believes Dennison is the right man for the job. Trump told reporters as much this afternoon in the Oval Office. His feet up on the Resolute Desk, a Diet Coke in one hand and a large fried chicken leg in the other, Trump mused that Fox News had "gotten the hint" and "kissed the ring."

"And that ring is on a very normal length ring finger, okay," Trump demanded of the press pool. "Don't go reportin' that my finger's all small and shit. That's fake news. Just ask my glove maker, Thumbelina. She says my hands are bigly yooge!"

JULY 9, 2019

British Ambassador Promises to Stop Having Opinions That Are Based in Fact

MERRY OLD LONDON TOWN IN JOLLY OLD ENG-UH-LAND — British Ambassador to the US, Kim Darroch, has found himself at the center of a swirling international controversy, based around leaked cables he sent regarding the Donald Trump presidential administration, and the president himself.

> "Britain's Ambassador to Washington has described Donald Trump as 'inept', 'insecure' and 'incompetent' in a series of explosive memos to Downing Street.
>
> "Sir Kim Darroch, one of Britain's top diplomats, used secret cables and briefing notes to impugn Trump's character, warning London that the White House was 'uniquely dysfunctional' and that the President's career could end in 'disgrace'. (Daily Mail)"

The cables contain what can only be described as embarrassing opinions that Darroch holds about Trump and his staff. The relationship

JULY

between the UK and the US has been strained of late already, and this incident could possibly cause more division between the White House and even conservatives in Great Britain. Darroch works for outgoing PM Theresa May, who has said in spite of the controversy over his cables that she still has "full confidence" in Darroch.

For his part, Trump has taken a few swipes at Darroch on Twitter.

There have been some calls from pro-Trump voices for Mr. Darroch to resign his post. It's unclear if he will do so, especially given May's very recent vocal support. However, at a press conference assembled in front of the Parliament building this morning, Darroch apologized profusely and promised to change his behavior permanently, to avoid this kind of scandal again.

"Primarily I want to say sorry to everyone for starting an international kerfuffle with my opinions," Darroch told reporters, "I should have remembered that the current occupant of the White House has skin so thin you can see his internal organs. While we may all admire the lofty paradigm of freedom of expression, there is a president who considers free speech a threat, and I must simply take that more into account before sending cables that contain my opinions."

Mr. Darroch solemnly promised to alter the way he arrives at his opinions, as well.

"I will no longer consider facts or evidence when forming an opinion," Darroch said. "Clearly we live in a time when facts are not as important as the feelings of some. Those feelings are so raw that it makes people get super-duper upset when you say things that are really

A LITTLE BIT LOUDER AND A WHOLE LOT WORSE

quite obvious to even the most casual of an observer. If I had sent a cable advising that water was still wet, would anyone be nearly as upset as when I called that man inept or incompetent?"

The White House has formally rejected Darroch's apologies and demanded that Queen Elizabeth punish him harshly for his "insults and transgressions of opinion."

"Maybe she can do one of those 'off with his head' things from *Alice in Wonderland*," President Trump was overheard suggesting to staff. "Or lock him up in the London Tower. He needs to pay for his crimes, and pay bigly."

JULY 9, 2019

Trump Warns His Enemies Not to Interfere in 2020 Election by Voting for the Democrats

WASHINGTON, D.C. — Though there are still several months left before the primary season comes to a close, President Donald Trump is already in full campaigning mode. Mr. Trump has taken swipes at Democratic candidate Vice President Joe Biden as well as the field in general. It's become obvious to even casual observers how important winning re-election is to the alleged billionaire and reality-TV host turned the most powerful man in the world.

This morning, speaking in the Oval Office to reporters, Trump addressed the issue of election security, and issued a warning to all of his "enemies, both foreign and, you know, here and stuff." The president's warning?

"Don't even think about meddling or interfering in our elections this time," Trump said emphatically, looking into the camera lenses and evoking memories of his time as host of NBC's *The Apprentice*. "I mean that. To all my enemies, both foreign and, you know, here and stuff — be warned. Do not tamper, interfere, meddle, or insert yourself into this election. We want it clean this time, okay? No funny business."

Reaching into the Resolute Desk for a Diet Coke, Trump popped it open, took a long belt from it, belched, and then continued.

"We're watching you like hawks; all of us are," Trump warned his enemies. "You even think about interfering with next year's election, and I will personally oversee your criminal trial if you attempt to in any way tamper with our election. Do not test me."

Trump opened another drawer in the desk and pulled out a bucket of KFC. The president pulled some chicken out and got out a bowl of gravy. Trump began dipping the chicken in the gravy as he continued to talk.

"Interfering in our election would really be a bigly bad move, so I hope all my enemies and haters are out there listening very carefully," Trump warned. "I'm not playing around. I'm not playing games. I'm in this fight for real, and I will be very vigilant!"

Before shooing the reporters out so he could have some "private executive time," Trump issued another threat to his enemies.

"Folks, don't test me on this one. I take election interference very seriously," Trump said. "So if we catch you interfering in my re-election by voting for the Democrat next year? You're going to jail. Big time in jail. I was going to sue you if you voted for someone other than me, but Stephen Miller has made a really convincing argument for why you should actually be sent to the concentration camps with the brown babies we kidnapped."

Speaker of the House Nancy Pelosi, a Democrat, told reporters upon hearing the word of Trump's threats that she is "so very very very upset, concerned, perturbed, and bothered" by it. However, she's unsure

JULY

if the American people want her to do anything. Pelosi said she's also not convinced she even has any powers to do anything.

"Look this is terrible. He's a lawless autocrat and he is doing real damage to our country's institutions," Pelosi said. "But doing something about it? Actually, doing something about it? Yikes, folks. Yikes. I'm not a big believer in inspiring your electorate to believe in you, and that's why I'm so proud of my approval rating never, ever, ever being above 30%, which is technically lower than Trump's, because I can't even manage to please my base like he can please his. The point is, doing stuff takes effort, which takes political courage, and once the results of a poll I've ordered conducted come back, I'll know whether it's politically expedient for me to do my job, okay? Great thanks. Remember — Mama Nancy knows better than you. ALWAYS."

JULY 10, 2019

NRA Backs Law Allowing Gun Sales After Shop Is Closed

FAIRFAX, VIRGINIA — The National Rifle Association has come out in favor of new legislation that would allow for the sale of firearms after a federally licensed retailer was closed for the day.

"Of course the NRA would prefer that there be no laws regarding firearms on the books because we know in our deeply patriotic hearts that guns are innocent, benign tools of peace," NRA deputy spokesman Cash Gachette told reporters this morning at a press conference announcing the proposed law, "but until this country is sufficiently uncucked, some losers are going to insist we be responsible about who gets to own a gun as if being responsible is even in the Second Amendment. So that being said, we want to show ourselves as supporting gun laws we consider to be common sense as well."

It's a "simple matter of freedom," Gachette said, that forces the NRA to support the new law.

"Why should you be forced to come back the next day to buy your gun, just because the shop has closed," Gachette asked rhetorically. "Shouldn't you be allowed to get your hands on a firearm whenever the hell you want to?"

JULY

The proposed law, which the NRA plans to help gun rights groups throughout all fifty states pursue in their legislatures, would give gun stores permission to sell firearms in their parking lots at all hours of the day. Supporters of the law say it gives prospective gun buyers a few more hours a day to secure a firearm. Critics say it opens up avenues for non-licensed sellers to hock their guns in parking lots and claim they're selling them on the up and up.

"Generally speaking, we support any law that makes it easier for anyone, literally anyone, to buy a gun," Gachette explained. "Why should we discriminate against stalkers, domestic abusers, and terrorists, just because they're seeking to take ownership of a tool that can kill us in an instant? That seems like the irrational fears of so-called educated people who so-called understand how so-called life actually so-called works. And that hurts our feelings deep down in our ammo hoarding hearts!"

The rate of incidence of mass shootings has not fallen since Donald Trump became president. In fact, in 2018 there were almost as many mass shooting incidents as there days. Gachette and the NRA wave off concerns that they are helping to foster an environment where fear drives gun sales more than facts and a sense of responsibility.

"When we conservatives talk about things like accountability and responsibility, we mean for poor people and people of color, or poor people of color, not gun owners," Gachette said. "The fact that you're out there buying a gun at all shows you have a sense of responsibility to protect yourself from the tyranny of government. I mean, sure, as a conservative I support the most oppressive forms of government control over your genitals and what drugs you take, but you get what I'm saying, fam."

The NRA will begin seeking cosponsors of their state bills sometime later this year, Gachette said.

JULY 18, 2019

Eric Trump: 95% of Unicorn Breeders Support His Father

NEW YORK, NEW YORK — In an interview on Fox News, President Donald Trump's smartest son not named Barron or Donald Jr. told viewers this morning that "well over 95% of unicorn breeders" in America support his father and want him re-elected.

"And let me ask your viewers this," Eric Trump asked the hosts of *Fox & Friends*, "What do you think our economy would be like if it weren't for the long hours and stressful work of our country's unicorn breeders? Dare I say they are the literal and economic backbone of the United States of America? I dare. I dare."

Eric says that "so many people love Daddy" that he always "draws massive crowds."

"Like at the bar in France when America won the World Cup," Eric said, "and they all started screaming our last name! It was so fun! And the best part is apparently all us Trumps are gonna get super duper laid because they just kept shouting about how much they want to fuck Trumps! Not only do we have the support of 95% of America's unicorn breeders; clearly we have the support of at least 206% of French people in France watching the World Cup at a bar!"

A LITTLE BIT LOUDER AND A WHOLE LOT WORSE

Eric also announced that he had decided to start an "unbiased, pro-Trump" polling company to get the "real feelings of real, white Americans to the real, white American people."

"Our first poll, conducted by Trump Polling, shows that not only does 95% of the country's unicorn breeding population love my daddy, more than 173% of people named Eric Trump think he's the BEST daddy," Eric said, shoving a spoonful of paste into his mouth. "And a full 561% of psychic Martian dog walkers from the planet Meepzorp are completely behind this MAGA agenda of ours!"

Since Eric concluded his Fox News interview, however, some controversy has arisen over his claims.

"Eric's a good kid, but his brain is basically a half-eaten jar of strawberry jelly," Jane Chestermeyer, the President of the American Unicorn Breeders Union, told reporters when asked about Eric's boasts. "He asked me last week if the AUBU would endorse his dad's campaign and I told him I knew the feelings of about 95% of our members on that subject. He took that to mean we'd endorse the president, but I was just trying to find a polite way to decline. I forgot temporarily the whole half-eaten jar of jelly brain thing."

JULY 26, 2019

Trump Campaign Manager Promises His Boss Will 'Keep America on the White Track'

CHANCHO BANCHO CANYON, ARIZONA — As he prepares the Donald Trump 2020 machine in Arizona — a state that has lost one of its Republican Senators since his boss took office — campaign manager Brad Parscale was seen coming out of a local grocery store. When approached by a reporter, he agreed to answer a few short questions as he loaded his food into the back of his car.

Mr. Parscale said he is "excited" to be involved in the 2020 campaign, and is "extremely, bigly proud:" of his achievements in the previous victory.

"We have to use words that the big guy uses like 'bigly' to make him feel less stupid," Parscale said as he put a bag of Doritos in the front passenger seat to snack on while he drove back to his hotel. "But when you're working for a doddering, old, entitled, spoiled trust fund racist and conman, dumbing your vocabulary down is one of the least terrible ways you sell yourself out for the sake of the almighty dollar, so it all comes out in the wash."

Mr. Parscale was asked if he thinks that President Trump can pull off a second historic victory. Parscale confidently assured the reporters

A LITTLE BIT LOUDER AND A WHOLE LOT WORSE

that his boss is capable of winning again. Trump's base has "come to really count on trust" him, Parscale thinks.

"That's because they know that Trump is the one guy to keep America on the white track," Parscale said. "He understands how important our heritage and culture are. You know, our heritage of white supremacy and our culture of subjugating and stealing things from people of color? That heritage and culture."

Parscale announced that the Trump campaign has "all sorts of fun events" planned leading up to next year's election.

"Tiki torch parades, book bonfires," Parscale listed, "just to name a couple. We're going to really emphasize the rally part in our campaign rallies. Maybe make Americans think of another kind of rally they've seen a bunch of angry, scared, racist white Americans attend before. Only this time, they don't have to worry about wearing hoods, because the MAGA hats do the same thing, and let us see their beautiful smiles, tooth and all."

AUGUST

AUGUST 1, 2019

Lahren: "Mermaids Are White, Just Like Santa and Jesus!"

LA CULERA RUBIA ARRUGADA, CALIFORNIA — Fox News contributing racist muppet Timothy Lahren railed against Disney's decision to cast a female of color in the central role of the upcoming live-action remake of 1989's animated classic, "The Little Mermaid," today.

Speaking on a conservative talk radio show, Ms. Limpbiskit told the show's host she thinks the casting of actress Halle Bailey was Disney "giving over to the angry left-wing mob of tolerance and representation." She went on to say that "changing the skin tone of established characters" is like "spitting in all our beautiful white faces." Thrombosis said that American conservatives should consider boycotting the new film when it comes out to "stand up for traditional skin colors and the heritage of white mermaids."

"This is just a crock of liberal, hippy-dippy, uber-PC, social Marxism bullcrap, and everyone knows it," LastCallForAlcohol said emphatically. "Because anyone who's educated even the slightest in mermology knows that merpeople are all white. Because they're made in God's image but crossed with a fish. And um, sorry libs, God's white, and we know he's white because his son, Jesus, was white too!"

Disney is "blackwashing mermaids just like liberals tried to blackwash Jesus" according to Ms. LolipopGuild.

"Everyone knows mermaids are white, just like Santa and Jesus," Tillamook said, "and all the blackwashing and fictional white character genocide in the world can't cover-up the truth! They might have the fact-based truth, but we have the truth that's in our hearts. The same heart in our chests that tells us Donald Trump is a super-successful, very rich, completely legitimately elected, popular president who has accomplished more than Barack Obama could in eight whole years is telling us that there is just no way in flipping hell that Ariel should be black."

Lompoc reminded the radio show's audience of another conservative controversy over whether Santa Claus can or should be black.

"Black Santa! Remember that? These liberals don't know how to stop stooping to new lows," Tabasco said. "No wonder these idiots believe in climate change! They think Santa Claus could be black somehow! Imagine that, not believing that there were weapons of mass destruction in Iraq, but believing Santa could be black! And they wonder why we make sure to cheat to win elections! We have to keep these loony morons out of office! Before they convince the fine people in red states that carbon dioxide is bad for the environment!"

Ms. Listeria gave listeners a list of other people that she will "never let the libtards blackwash."

AUGUST

"Some people might think I'm unaware of how racist I am, or whatever, but I will not sit idly by while liberals blackwash everyone from Marty McFly to Luke Skywalker to James Bond," Lamplight said. "That's just not how I roll, fam! What's next, them stealing jazz, rock and roll, hip hop, and marijuana back from us? I don't think so!"

AUGUST 14, 2019

Tucker Carlson: "It's Not Racist If I Call Them the N-Word in My Head"

NEW YORK, NEW YORK — Right-wing pundit and Fox News lead white supremacy anchor Tucker Carlson told a talk radio host this morning that he's "sick and tired" of being called a white supremacist "just because racist words come out of [his] mouth."

"I've had it up to the point of my hood with these baseless attacks on my character," Carlson told W-KKK's Nate Bedford during morning drive time today, "and frankly, the simple fact is that if they never *hear* me calling them racial epithets, then for all intents and purposes I'm not racist."

Carlson shocked Mr. Bedford when he said that he was incorrect to classify white supremacy was a "hoax" last week.

"I should've said, 'White supremacy is awesome and the idea that it's somehow bad for America or western society is a hoax,'" Carlson explained. "I mean, were whites not the supreme race in this country when we won the Revolutionary War? Were we not the dominant race when the Constitution was written? It seems to me like white supremacy was the way America got great in the first place, thanks to all the free labor from the blacks and Chinese. But who had the smarts

AUGUST

to reduce their labor costs so much? That's right, we whites."

Mr. Carlson admits that he thinks "blacks are just by nature more poor and violent" and that "whites just figured it out first and better," but that he hasn't "done the one thing that racists do."

"I've never called anyone the n-word. Out loud. I mean, sure, I've done it in my head every time an uppity one is standing in line at the grocery store before me, and I want to cut in line because I'm white and they won't let me," Carlson said, "or when I just, you know, see one being all urban-y and not showing full respect for my white accomplishments."

If people of color never hear him use racial epithets, Carlson figures that means he's "not really racist."

"If a tree falls in the woods, is fashioned into a cross, lit on fire, and put in my URBAN neighbor's yard, but no one's around to catch me, does that make me racist? Of course not," Tucker said. "Likewise, it's not racist if I call them the n-word in my head!"

Since Carlson's declaration that white supremacy and white nationalism are a hoax, there have been calls to boycott his shows' sponsors. Carlson waves those threats off.

"What, you think I can't find other sponsors? I happen to know of a very prestigious, historic organization that said they'll be a permanent sponsor of my show," Carlson announced, "and let's just say I know I can trust this klan's word. I'm sure I'm white about this one."

AUGUST 14, 2019

Evangelical Libertarian: "Jesus Died on the Cross to End Progressive Taxation"

HOLY OAK, VIRGINIA — Televangelist Bill Millen makes no bones about it. He loves "God, guns, America, Jesus, and President Trump's trace rectal elements."

"If the president cuts one, I will volunteer to bury my Godly nose in his ungodly a-hole, because I know two things," Millen recently told his tell congregants. "One — God sent his only begotten son, Jesus, to this Earth to wash away our sins and teach us how to spot and remove a libtard. Second of off, and this one is big, he sent us Donald Trump to bring this country back closer to His vision for it. Here's a hint: watch *The Handmaid's Tale*. We want that to be a documentary, instead of a tease like it is now."

Millen says that lately he's been "seeing and hearing about far too many so-called liberal Christians" and their attempts to push for more progressive agendas, using the teachings of Christ to validate that push.

"Excuse me? Love your neighbors? What kind of crap is that? Sure Jesus said, but he didn't mean it the way these liberal so-called Christians mean it," Millen insisted. "He meant to, like, love them, but first make sure they were born here and not mooching off you like some

AUGUST

kind of midwest farmer, fam!"

What's really disturbing to Rev. Millen, however, is when he sees people trying to use Jesus as an excuse to tax the wealthy.

"For some reason, every beta Christian comes at me with the, 'Pay to Caesar what is due Caesar' thing," Millen said, "and I'm sorry, but that's crap. Pure crap. Sure, Jesus said you can't take it all with you. Sure, he said faith without works doesn't cut it. And sure, he said it's easier to shove a camel through a needle's eye than it is for a rich man to get into heaven. So what? None of that matters."

Rev. Millen told his flock that a former president helped modern-day Christians "throw off" interpretations of the Bible that "don't support the good, clean, almighty and holy free market."

"Jesus died to save us from our sins, sure. But we all remember what St. Ronald Ignatius Reagan's administration was able to find in the back of the Bible," Millen said, "near the appendix, don't we? They proved that Jesus died on the cross to end progressive taxation."

Millen challenged "stupid moron libtard cuck wannabe Christians" to defend taxation in a biblical sense.

"Yes, Jesus wanted us to take care of the poor and sick, but did he want us to make everyone slaves to the government," Millen asked rhetorically, "which is literally what happens when you help someone keep their lights on, or put food in their hungry kid's stomachs? Go on, libs, defend slavery. Because that's what taxation is. I wish it said it in the Bible, but we can definitely pretend it does like we do with literally everything else our political ideology says that contradicts what's

A LITTLE BIT LOUDER AND A WHOLE LOT WORSE

actually in the Bible."

AUGUST 19, 2019

Scientists Can Finally Prove Which Trump Can Outsmart a Bag of Hammers

After years of speculation and wonder, scientists at a leading research lab have published a study that they say supports a formula the team wrote for determining which member of the Trump family is smarter than a bag of hammers. The question of whether President Donald Trump or any of the people related to him are more or less intelligent than a sack filled to the brim with hammers, or even rocks, has long been a question that scientists around the globe attempted to answer. While a 2008 study gave researchers insights into whether the Trump klan was smarter than a bowl of pudding, comparing their intellect to a large bag full of hammers was always considered to be a question too difficult for modern tools and techniques.

That is until the University of Northwest Eastern Ohio of Pennsylvania's bio-research department released their report entitled, "Are There Any Trumps Who Can Outwit a Bag of Hammers?" Now, the team who conducted the landmark study has begun to do TV and radio interviews, explaining their findings. This morning, Dr. Carol Malloy, the woman who headed up the team, discussed the study on W-FRT in Kentucky.

A LITTLE BIT LOUDER AND A WHOLE LOT WORSE

"What we found was an equation for determining if a Trump, or someone who is sleeping with a Trump, is smarter or dumber than a bag of hammers," Dr. Malloy said. "We even were able to write a formula for people who are both — related to a Trump and sleeping with him. We call it the Ivanka Theorem."

It doesn't matter what kind of hammers are in the bag, or what the bag is made of, Malloy said. Neither factored into the results, she said.

"Whether it's a burlap sack of sledgehammers, or a plastic bag full of claw hammers," Malloy said, "our formula works the same every time. No matter what. The results are more predictable than a racist rant from a Fox News host."

Malloy told the radio host this morning that the formula for verifying whether a Trump is smarter than a bag of hammers is actually more reliable and consistent in its results than other, much more famous scientific equations.

"It turns out, we came up with the Pythagorean theory of Trump stupidity," Malloy said. "Except there's no squaring of A, B, or C involved. Or any math, really. What we determined is that you don't even need math, or even to use the scientific method!"

Dr. Malloy explained further.

"All you really need to do is verify that you're being asked if a Trump is dumber or smarter than a box of rocks," Malloy said. "Every Trump, every single one of them, is dumber than a bag of hammers. If you ask our team, there are two constants in the known universe — change, and the stupidity of the Trump family."

AUGUST

President Trump has reportedly vowed to avenge his family's honor, in light of the news.

"First of off, everyone knows I'm smarter than every hammer out there because it's in the Constitution, okay? It says right there, in bold, under the part about God or guns or some bullshit," Trump yelled at reporters, "It says, 'President Trump, not just any president, PRESIDENT TRUMP, is smarter than everyone and everything, including a bag of hammers, so shut up you libtarded idiot radical Bob Mueller Democrats or you'll get put in the Mexican concentration camps.' It says it. Right there. Plain as day. Why would I lie? I never lie! I was just telling George Washington and Elvis the other day how much I don't lie, and they told me they believed me."

AUGUST 24, 2019

Trump Calls Domino's Pizza "the Enemy of the People" for Forgetting His Hot Wing Dipping Sauce

WASHINGTON, D.C. — The list of people, businesses, and government officials who President Donald Trump has referred to as an "enemy of the people" is growing so long, some on the Hill have suggested Americans may have to start keeping a list of people he hasn't given that label to, as it would be a much shorter list to maintain. Today at lunch, Mr. Trump launched a blistering verbal barrage at a new target — Domino's Pizza — and forgetting the most powerful man in the free world's dipping sauce for his hot wings might cost the food chain dearly.

"I hereby order Domino's Pizza to come to the White House immediately, with lots and lots of free pizzas," Trump commanded via Twitter. "You must atone for your most egregious and unbelievable insult to me!"

Just minutes later, Trump tweeted an attack on Dominoes again.

"Forgetting dipping sauces, Domino's Pizza? Are you kidding me," Trump demanded, "and here I thought the media, Democrats, people who don't like me generally, and that one daughter of mine, Not Ivanka, were the Enemy of the People. But your pizza hoodlums are too! You

AUGUST

are the enemy of the people!"

Reportedly, last night President Trump was routinely ending his day; four large pizzas, Fox News on the TV, and his First Lady by his side, in the presidential bedroom. Except, last night the pizzas also included hot wings because, as one source close to the situation put it, "Donald really loves hot wings." All did end well for the president and his First Lady, however, when he noticed that the pizza delivery driver had not delivered the hot wings with any dipping sauces.

"No ranch?! No bleu cheese? IVANKA! IVANKA," Trump shouted and nudged his First Lady, "THEY FUCKING FORGOT MY DIPPING SAUCES! How the hell am I supposed to enjoy my hot wings if I can't dip them in a variety of savory sauces that both cool the burn of the wing sauce, but also enhance the overall depth of flavor of said hot wings, IVANKA?!"

The First Lady was unable to console Mr. Trump. No matter what she tried, even things that we are legally prohibited from reprinting because we're not sure what the laws on incest are if both parties are way, way old enough to know how disgusting it is — and frankly they are — worked. The president was completely unhinged.

"FIRST THING TOMORROW MORNING, IVANKA, I AM SUMMONING THE HEAD OF DOMINO's PIZZA HERE, TO THE WHITE HOUSE," Trump shouted, "BECAUSE I AM PRESIDENT AND YOU DO NOT FORGET THE PRESIDENT'S DIPPING SAUCES!"

When Mr. Trump began his workday at his usual 11:00 am today,

A LITTLE BIT LOUDER AND A WHOLE LOT WORSE

having completed his scheduled six hours of "executive time," he picked up the phone and called the local Domino's franchise personally.

"Hello? Hello? Hi, this is your favorite president of all time," Trump began. The woman on the other end said something that made him recoil with horror. "No! Not that urban guy! ME! TRUMP! It's Trump! Look, sweetheart, do me a favor and put Bob Domino on the horn would you? I gotta tell Bob Domino that his delivery guy fucked up something bigly."

When the Domino's employee told President Trump no one named Bob Domino worked there, or at any Domino's restaurant she knew of, he became irate. He demanded to speak to her supervisor, and the employee obliged. But the supervisor had the same message for President Trump — Bob Domino didn't exist. Trump didn't believe what he was being told.

"I'm sorry, but I don't believe what I'm being told," Trump said, growing agitated. "My closest advisers, who I pay insane amounts of money to never disappoint me, ever, told me that Bob Domino runs Domino's Pizza after I asked them one night, 'Hey, is the guy who runs Domino's Pizza named Bob Domino because I think it is?' And they confirmed it. They never lie because I never lie, and I don't tolerate lies being told in front of me."

Trump then rattled off a series of lies he doesn't believe.

"Climate change? Lie. Chinese hoax lie. Crooked's popular vote margin? Lies. Democrat lies. Bob Mueller 2.3 million angry Democrat lies," Trump said, stamping his feet as he paced around the Resolute

AUGUST

Desk. "Historically low approval ratings? Lies. Mathematical lies. And Bob Domino doesn't exist? LIES. PIZZA LIES. AND THERE IS NOTHING THAT MAKES ME SADDER THAN PIZZA LIES!"

That's when the president decided to use Twitter to demand that Domino's Pizza's executives come to the White House urgently, and with as many free pizzas as they can put in their cars. After sending his tweeted ultimatum, Trump put his iPhone down. He reached inside his desk, into a special drawer that he keeps KFC chicken in. The drawer is restocked several times during the day by White House staff. Trump ate the chicken as he sat down behind the desk once more.

"The trap is set! Now, when those Domino's cucks show up, and Bob Domino is with them, I'll arrest the whole company for lying to a president," Trump said, "which is, like, totally in the Constitution, or at least I pretend it is and Bill Barr said that's good enough for him."

Representatives from Domino's have not responded to the president's demands, or to a request for a comment on this story.

AUGUST 25, 2019

Man Chanting 'Send Her Back' Can't Locate His Home State on a Map

COLD CAVE HILLS, TENNESSEE — Last night, right-wing podcaster, commentator, and singer/writer Jethro Bohiggins was among the crowd at President Donald Trump's MAGA rally. Though he lives hundreds of miles away in another state, Bohiggins says it was a "no brainer" decision for him to hop in his 1989 Ford sedan and drive up to North Carolina to attend the rally. Bohiggins was among those who gleefully chanted "Send her back" when Trump brought up Minnesota congresswoman Rep. Ilhan Omar's name.

"It was one of the best moments I've ever had as a pure, white, good, clean, all American patriot," Bohiggins told listeners today on his podcast. "Nothing says freedom, liberty, and independence like shouting at a brown person to leave your country because you're offended by the words that come out of their mouth! And if those words are all namby-pamby, hippie-dippie crap about letting people be free to choose their own, best life, then that's even better! True freedom is doing what the GOP and its orange savior tell us to do, is it not fam?"

Bohiggins says that the chanting reminded him "very much" of some of his favorite times as an American.

"It's like when you're lightin' up a big ol' wooden lowercase T, for Trump, on some uppity urban's lawn, and you and your, um, clan, start spontaneously whistlin' Dixie and chanting, 'Jews will not replace us!'," Bohiggins ranted, "Or when we were burning all those copies of the Koran and the AP U.S. history textbooks! There's just something very American about mobs and chanting stuff about brown people that makes the bald eagle in my heart soar!"

As much fun as he had at the rally, Jethro says things took a little bit of a downward turn as he was driving back home.

"See, the problem, fam, is that I'm not a cuck, so I refuse to have one of those smartphones. We all know you only get so-called smart in so-called schools, and schools are where libtards indoctrinate us, so I don't need nothin' that's smart in my life," Bohiggins explained, "not no smartphone. Not no smart TVs. Not no smart president. I like my shit easy and dumb, fam!"

Because he doesn't own a smartphone, Jethro was left to rely on maps to navigate himself from the rally in North Carolina, back to his home state of Tennessee. But, there was one problem with that, as well.

"I also don't buy no books, ever, because for the same reasons! Books mean education, which means libtard indoctrination, so I don't buy any Thomas Guides or nothin'," Jethro said. "The problem was that I guess I had accidentally used my map as a napkin when I stopped off at the Chick-Fil-A. See, napkins for customers only and I was just there to rub one out. Point is, I lost my map, fam, and I was stuck for a good long while in North Carolina."

A LITTLE BIT LOUDER AND A WHOLE LOT WORSE

Without his map, Jethro says that he was "utterly and completely lost," and he was forced to break from his principles and buy a new map. However, Bohiggins wasn't out of hot water, even with the map. There was one more problem he was left with.

"I tried every way I could to find Tennessee on a map, but not being able to read, that put me in one hell of a bind," Bohiggins said. "I mean, I know we ain't the mitten-shaped state, and I know where Commiefornia is because of all the pipe bombs I've sent them over the years. But I couldn't for the life of me find Tennessee on a map, and I had to pick up a hitchhiker."

The hitchhiker, thankfully, had a smartphone with GPS.

"I still ain't gonna buy one for myself, but yeah, I'm glad we were able to get back home, eventually," Jethro told his audience. "Because it's much easier to make memes about how un-American and bad for the country Ilhan Omar is from home, which makes not being able to find your way home even tougher to get through. I did it though. All on my own, just like a good conservative does."

A caller asked Bohiggins how he did it alone if he admitted he needed a stranger's smartphone, eventually.

"ALL BY MYSELF, FAM," Bohiggins shouted. "And Omar can still go back where she came from, and as soon as I learn how to read, and then subsequently learn where her birth country is, I'll personally send her packing there...once I get off the dole and back working, fam. I promise. Which reminds me, hit me up on my Patreon or Venmo or Paypal. I need some Skoal and a pregnancy test because we think my

AUGUST

wife is pregnant, and ever since I met her when she was born, I knew I'd make a baby with my cousin Rita."

AUGUST 25, 2019

Mexican Government Releases Detailed Audit of How Much They've Paid for Trump's Wall so Far

MEXICO CITY, MEXICO — The federal government of Mexico has published an extremely detailed audit of just how much of its budget has been allocated and spent on the border wall between the United States and their country. Along with the audit, Mexico's government issued a warning to the Trump administration that they "might have some problems doing the math" contained inside it.

"Not because the math is all that complicated, of course," the letter states, "but because your trade war with China showed us you don't live in mathematical reality. But, if you have one of your smarter children, one of the ones you don't have lustful feelings for, not the one with your name, and not the one that looks more like an 80's action star with the first name Gary. Ask either the female one you don't say disgusting things about. Maybe she can operate a calculator."

During the 2016 presidential campaign season, Mr. Trump promised his supporters that that building a new wall on the southern border would be a top priority. Infamously, he also promised that Mexico would pay for the wall. It was a guarantee he doubled, tripled, quadrupled and more on. At rally after rally, Trump promised the crowd

AUGUST

Mexico would pay for the wall.

It's unclear even how much the wall has been completed since Trump took office. The administration points to a "whole lot of WD-40 has been sprayed on gate hinges" as evidence of "major progress" toward keeping Trump's promise. Mexico has not paid for any of it, either. In the time since Trump was sworn in, Mexico has on occasion offered to pay for a pizza party to celebrate Trump's personal lawyer going to jail for lying to Congress, and to pay for Trump's therapy sessions.

Weighing in at just over one single page, Mexico's audit is exhaustive, if not extremely brief.

"We didn't need to waste much paper printing the report," Mexico's letter explains, "because as you can see, there isn't anything to report. Contrary to what the American people were told, Mexico has not paid anything for the wall. However, in the interest of making sure nothing is lost in translation, we have taken the time to find a few English synonyms for the amount Mexico has paid, and ever will pay, for Mr. Trump's wall."

In all, Mexico lists twenty-five different ways to say "zero."

"None, zilch, squat, bupkus," Mexico wrote, "these are some of the classic ways you say it in your language. But in any language, the math is quite undeniable. We have paid absolutely nothing toward the wall, and we will continue to spend at the exact same pace for the duration of forever."

President Trump was reportedly on his D.C area golf course, doing

A LITTLE BIT LOUDER AND A WHOLE LOT WORSE

what aides call "the least damaging thing he can do as president." According to Trump, he was shooting 32 strokes under par when he got the news of Mexico's audit. Reportedly, Trump threw his entire golf bag off the cart and flopped around on the ground, crying for a moment or two before collecting himself and being driven off the course by his caddy.

SEPTEMBER

SEPTEMBER 5, 2019

Trump Hereby Orders Every State to Change Its Name to "Alabama"

WASHINGTON, D.C. — The other 49 states in the union have exactly one week to "do whatever bullshit their constitutions require" that will change their names officially to "Alabama," according to a new order given by President Donald J. Trump.

"I hereby order each and every state in the country to do whatever bullshit their constitutions require and change their names to Alabama," Trump shouted as he stuck his head out of the Oval Office doorway, expecting staff to take notes and send the order to the fifty state legislatures and governors' mansions throughout the U.S. "They have one week to comply, or I nuke them like a hurricane on my bad side!"

Trump explained that "no one, not even the most perfect president ever" could make the mistake of announcing the wrong state was in the pathway of a deadly hurricane if all the states are named the same.

"Think about it! This might be my best idea since Trump Steaks! It's quite simple, really," Trump said emphatically when asked about the order later on the White House lawn. "It might be my best idea since opening a casino! Hell, I daresay it might be my best idea since starting my own university!"

A LITTLE BIT LOUDER AND A WHOLE LOT WORSE

The White House believes naming each state "Alabama" will have a multitude of positive effects for the president, politically and otherwise.

"We're pretty sure that means the president will receive every state's Electoral College votes next year," one administration official told us. "And that's to say nothing about how excited many of his supporters will be to finally know all fifty state capitals!"

Some other names were considered, our source tells us.

"We were thinking of calling every state 'Trump,' but thought would require more Sharpies and more weather maps, so we went with Alabama instead," the source said.

Though generally the feeling in the White House is that naming every state Alabama will be good in the long run, some issues just will never be solved because of it, worry some officials.

"I mean, the simple fact is that most people in Alabama still won't be able to spell it, even when it's right there in front of them on every other state," one aide said, "but what can you do?"

Thus far, there has been no official response from the states. Legal scholars have suggested that while what Trump did was unconstitutional, as long as his personal attorney William Barr says it's okay, it probably is. Speaker of the House Nancy Pelosi was seen running to her car and shouting with her fingers firmly in her ears.

SEPTEMBER 14, 2019

NRA Supports Universal Background Checks and Waiting Periods for Vaping Products

FAIRFAX, VIRGINIA — During a press conference this morning, a spokesterrorist for the National Rifle Association announced that the NRA officially backs the Trump administration's reported effort to ban flavored e-cigarettes due to the sudden outbreak of lung illnesses related to the practice of vaping. However, during the same presser, it was revealed that the NRA supports other measures if an outright ban is not instituted.

"As everyone who knows anything about us knows," NRA Junior Deputy Media Liaison Cash Gachette told reporters today, "the NRA is extremely concerned about the well-being of children. That's why we advocate so tirelessly for a world in which every child grows up literally surrounded on all sides by guns. And while the NRA has traditionally been very much so against the prohibition of things in the past, we realized this prohibition would, and I cannot stress this enough, not impact gun sale profit margins, and therefore, we didn't care about it all that much."

Gachette told the media the NRA backs the Trump administration "completely and fully no matter what" due to "certain shared friendships and partnerships around the globe."

"Let's just say that we have similar comrades in the Kremlin," Gachette said with a wink. "Know what I mean? Let's just say we won't be RUSSIAN away from President Trump any time soon, get it?"

Gachette winked again.

"But if the administration decides to go a different route, and let's say they decide a full ban is unnecessary," Gachette explained, "the NRA fully backs efforts to institute universal background checks for all vaping products. After all, don't we want to make sure our kids can't get their hands on such deadly devices? These aren't benign implements of peace and love like an AR-15! These are killing machines, and I for one am glad that the Trump administration is doing what they can to keep our kids safe."

Mr. Gachette reiterated several times that the NRA backs Trump's regulations because "American lives are at stake."

"Six entire Americans have died from this deadly threat to our health safety, and we cannot let such an outrageous death toll continue," Gachette said.

The NRA also would support efforts to force a waiting period into effect for any and all vaping-related purchases.

"Who knows? Maybe we can save a lung or two by making people wait a week," Gachette wondered aloud, "Maybe if they have time to really think about what it is they're doing, they'll reconsider. I mean, they're not just waltzing into a WalMart and buying a shotgun for god's sake! They're buying a personal vice that has so far killed far fewer kids

SEPTEMBER

than guns, or even have died in ICE custody this year! We're just glad the administration is moving so swiftly. These aren't first graders turned into Swiss cheese by a semi-automatic rifle; these are mostly older people with chronic health problems, to begin with, and we all know the Constitution's thoughts on subjects like these!"

When asked about a recent report that a California vape producer is starting to give away AR-15 assault rifles with purchases of their cartridges, Gachette said the NRA is "keeping a close eye" on the situation.

"We love anything that involves large numbers of guns being purchased," Gachette said. "That means promotions, giveaways, police departments, civil wars, whatever. We just want more guns bought with dollars. We don't even really care if it's the same sixteen people in a bunker in Alabama buying all the guns. We just want money. Let me reiterate that because it's absolutely vital to the survival of the republic. We just want money."

SEPTEMBER 20, 2019

Fearing Another Whistleblower, President Bans Tea Kettles From White House

WASHINGTON, D.C. — This morning, the President of the United States issued an edict, demanding that all whistles and things that can whistle be removed from the White House grounds "immediately and without any bigly delays." President Trump Trump specifically banned teapots and tea kettles from the White House as well.

"I won't stand for it! I will not stand for any more whistleblowing in administration," Trump shouted at reporters in the Oval Office today. "That's why I have ordered all the teapots taken out of this place. If I had known they'd snitch on me, I would've been drinking coffee this whole time. You never heard of a coffee pot whistleblowing on anyone, have you?"

Mr.Trump has found himself this week at the center of yet another firestorm of controversy. Reportedly, a whistleblower at an intelligence agency was so unnerved by a promise they say Mr. Trump made to a foreign leader that they filed a whistleblower complaint. The White House and Department of Justice have been working to block the complaint from becoming public. Federal law allows the whistleblower to go straight to Congress in such an even as being blocked by the

SEPTEMBER

executive branch.

"Honestly, I'm not even sure why any American thinks they can stop me from making whatever promises to whomever I want to," Trump yelled. "Bill Barr, my personal Attorney General, told me that pretty much the Constitution says I can think, say, and most importantly do anything I want to. So, I'm not even sure why me trying to openly collude with a foreign government again is even being discussed in a way that implies I'm not allowed to literally do everything I want. But I assure you, Barr will be here shortly to wag his finger and smugly insist he's right, no matter how illogical it is for a country without monarchy to have a kingly president."

Mr. Trump angrily blasted "everyone who didn't warn" him about the "dangers of whistles to presidents."

"Nobody fucking told me I should be careful about whistling and whistlers," Trump said. "I mean, whenever I fart, my a-hole whistles! Is my a-hole going to snitch on me now? Is my a-hole going to go and tattle like a little beotch, as that whistleblower did? Also, for the record, a-hole means my asshole!"

Beginning immediately, White House staff have been directed to take any and all teapots or kettles from the building and "throw them in the same fires we burned all those books in," Trump said, referring to the book bonfires he holds every weekend with Stephen Miller.

"I don't want any whistling being done around here. Period. If whistling is what's going to get me impeached, then by God no one and nothing is gonna be whistling around here," Trump bellowed. "I'm not even gonna let Miller whistle 'Dixie' around here anymore, no matter how catchy a tune that is!"

Moments later, Trump accused the Obama administration of "forcing" him to hire his own team of people, one of which "snitched like a big ol' ass" on him, he said.

"I'm fairly sure, and Bill Barr says this is absolutely true if it comes out of my word hole, that Obama pulled some dirty Democrat Sharia Voodoo on me," Trump said. "He forced me to appoint my own national security and intelligence team, one of whom obviously turned on me and snitched like a big ol' ass! And I will not stand for this!"

Before chasing the reporters out of the Oval Office, Trump stated that he "shouldn't have even had to" demand the White House be stripped of whistles and whistling things.

"Again, let me just say this one more time," Trump yelled. "Nobody has the right to tell me what to do, or what to say. But more importantly, nobody has the right to hold me accountable for what I end up saying and doing. I AM PRESIDENT! A very narrow group of people in three states gave me barely just enough votes to win, which automatically makes me your God-Emperor King! It's in the Constitution, and even if it isn't? Who cares! Barr will back me up, and my base will gleefully treat me like royalty as long as I keep saying things like, "Ooga Booga socialism. So really, let's just cut the bullshit and hand me a crown and scepter because this whole voting thing is dumb and a waste of time, frankly."

SEPTEMBER 25, 2019

John Adams Once Called the King of England for Dirt on Thomas Jefferson

While the nation's political and governmental institutions grapple with an authentic constitutional crisis, debating the possible impeachment of President Donald Trump, historians have unearthed and publicized the discovery of new evidence that he might not the first Commander in Chief to seek foreign help in an upcoming election.

The National Academy of History Seekers, or NAHS, is one of the oldest established consortiums of historians. Founded in 1819, NAHS and its historians have endeavored to accurately document the history of the United States. At a press conference today, NAHS Senior Junior Executive Deputy Historian Carol Caruthers announced the discovery of primary source materials that indicate John Adams called the King of England to see if he could get "dirt" on Thomas Jefferson, who he was running against in an upcoming election at the time.

"Our office clerk Billy Williamson was going through some boxes in our 'Old AF' bin — it's the bin where keep all the stuff that's old as fuck, you see — and he found a phone bill from the late 18th century," Ms. Caruthers told reporters. "Obviously this would have been a major scandal even in 1800. There were, after all, already provisions in the

A LITTLE BIT LOUDER AND A WHOLE LOT WORSE

Constitution that prevented such an abuse of power. That's why it would appear, then-President John Adams ordered this phone bill to be hidden away, hopefully never to be seen again."

Caruthers says that NAHS can confirm what the content of the phone call was, thanks to some sleuthing detective work from their team.

"We already had a journal entry from Adams that admitted to a 'rather unique and interesting exchange' he says he had with the King of England," Caruthers said. "Adams wrote that he and the King agreed that they had a mutual interest in draining the swamp — a literal swamp that England and the U.S. were both disputing ownership of. They also both agreed it was necessary to investigate Thomas Jefferson, who would go on to defeat Adams in the general election that year, making Adams the first single-term president in our nation's history."

The NAHS cannot confirm whether or not the King of England or then-President Adams exchanged anything other than the one phone call. Caruthers says she too is "blown away" that Adams was not only hiding the phone call, but also the fact that he had telephone technology at his disposal already.

"Though that's also pretty easily explained when you realize that Adams had been accidentally visited by Wyld Stalyns during their excellent adventure through time," Caruthers said. "Whether it was Bill S. Preston, Esq, or Ted "Theodore" Logan, someone got Adams that technology, and he used it. How the King of England got it? Well, I'm not writing this dumb fucking satire piece, am I? Ask that tubby fuck

SEPTEMBER

flailing his fingers at the keyboard right now."

Ms. Caruthers was suddenly yanked out of the press conference shouting.

"See," Caruthers yelled, "this is his fault! He sent these goons after me! And now he's stealing a plot device from a John Candy movie called *Delirious*. You should watch it! It's great! Better than this derivative garbage!"

SEPTEMBER 27, 2019

Gingrich Explains Subtle Differences Between Consensual Blowjobs and Coercing Foreign Governments to Investigate Political Rivals

WASHINGTON, D.C. — In 1998, Newt Gingrich was the Speaker of the House in the United States House of Representatives.

A Republican, Gingrich was famously one of the loudest voices in Congress pushing for a special prosecutor, investigation, impeachment, and — he had hoped — removal from office of President William Jefferson Clinton. At the center of the impeachment, the push was the fact that Clinton had lied under oath about a consensual sexual relationship he'd had with an intern on his staff, Monica Lewinsky. Gingrich and his party argued at the time that obstruction of justice, even in a case that involved lying about personal and private sex acts between consenting adults, rises to the level of the "high crimes or misdemeanors" that the Constitution sets as its only bar for removing a sitting president.

Some have noticed that Gingrich, who pressed for impeachment at least partially on moral and ethical grounds, was not so keen to criticize President Donald Trump, even though it's now confirmed that Trump's lawyer facilitated a payment of $130,000 to porn star Stormy Daniels in exchange for her silence about her sexual affair with Trump. The

SEPTEMBER

payment came toward the end of the 2016 presidential election and some legal experts have posited that it could constitute an illegal use of campaign funds.

Ms. Daniels sued Trump in court, saying that since he didn't sign the non-disclosure agreement it was null and void. Later, Daniels' attorney said that Trump had "further threatened" his client. Thus far, there have not been any congressional Republicans willing to go so far as Gingrich went during the Clinton administration. Mr. Gingrich never called Trump out in anywhere near the same terms as he did with Clinton's sexual indiscretions.

Perhaps even more eyebrow-raising is the fact that Gingrich has defended Trump in the face of the former's own impeachment crisis. Mr. Trump, feeling emboldened by the lack of concrete accountability in the face of the Mueller Report's well-documented potential abuses of power, attempted to collude with the new President of Ukraine. However, a whistleblower complaint about those attempts and other abuses of executive power have brought Speaker of the House Nancy Pelosi out of hibernation, and Trump now faces his own impeachment peril.

Today, Gingrich appeared on a conservative talk radio show and explained what he called "the numerous subtle but important differences between consensual blowjobs and open collusion with foreign governments to subvert our democracy." The show's host promised Mr. Gingrich that if he could explain his thinking well enough, he'd send him a gift certificate for a deep-fried cheeseburger

A LITTLE BIT LOUDER AND A WHOLE LOT WORSE

from his favorite deep-fried cheeseburger restaurant.

Gingrich said he "relished" the opportunity to explain his thinking both back in the nineties and now.

"Absolutely, I'll take that deal, because I've been hearing a lot of people criticize me for what they think is my hypocrisy on this issue," Gingrich said. "But the truth is that there is a very subtle nuance to the difference between President Clinton and President Trump's situations."

The host told Gingrich to take all the time he needed. Gingrich thanked him, took a deep breath, and spoke."

"Bill Clinton was a Democrat, Donald Trump is a Republican," Gingrich declared. "There, I've explained it, can I have that deep-fried cheeseburger now?"

OCTOBER

OCTOBER 5, 2019

Jim Jordan: "We Can't Impeach Trump Before Impeaching Joe Biden"

WASHINGTON, D.C. — Rep. Gym Jordan told reporters this morning that he "absolutely does not and will not ever" support the impeachment of President Donald J. Trump.

"Look, I don't care if he shoots my mother on 5th Avenue. I don't care if he literally sells our country to Russian oligarchs. Hell, I don't even care if he's a serial sexual abuser of college wrestlers," Jordan said today at a press conference. "Turning and looking the other way is something I'm sort of really good at."

But, Jordan said, he cannot "simply look the other way" when it comes to impeaching someone else — former Vice President Joe Biden.

"What I want to know, though, truly, is why we are even remotely talking about impeaching Trump when we haven't discussed impeaching Joe Biden first," Jordan demanded, with anger and emotion flaring in his voice. "

Jordan ripped Biden for "standing by and letting Trump take the fall for things" Biden didn't do based on things that the public now knows Trump did think Biden did.

"This is all a deep state plot for Hillary Clinton to lose to Donald

A LITTLE BIT LOUDER AND A WHOLE LOT WORSE

Trump so that he could be impeached and Joe Biden would be elected," Jordan insisted. "This is so plain and obvious. I almost feel bad for the Democrats that they think a president can't just pressure whoever he wants to win an election. I mean, c'mon, what do you think, that you don't live in an imperial monarchy? Get with the program, libs!"

Rep. Jordan called on Biden to "give himself up" and submit to an impeachment inquiry led not by Jordan in any official capacity, but by himself, and former Congressmen Darrell Issa and Trey Gowdy.

"Trey, Darrell, and I are gonna get to the bottom of all this. And it probably ends up in us impeaching not just Joe Biden, but Crooked Hillary Clinton," Jordan shouted. "Hell, I'll impeach the whole damn Democrat Party, rank and file voters too! In fact, if you're a registered member of the Democratic Party, I would warn you right now, we're gonna impeach you."

Whether or not Biden or Clinton, or even rank and file Democrats, are or have been president or even held an office, that is impeachable, is not of any concern to Jordan, he said.

"Since when did Republican politicians have to deal in anything remotely resembling reality? Trickle-down economics works. There were weapons of mass destruction in Iraq," Jordan rambled. "Hillary sold 890% of our uranium stocks to Russia, then turned around and forced Trump to collude with Russia, all in effort to cover-up Benghazi for George Soros and the Bob Mueller angry Democrats. This is so clear to see that I question anyone who doesn't see it, frankly. And they'll be impeached too!"

OCTOBER

Mr. Biden has already responded by telling Jordan he can "go fuck himself."

"Oh, Gym wants me to submit to some non-existent authority he has over me," Biden asked. "Here, let me tell you a hilarious 50-year-old anecdote about me, a segregationist, and a rabbi. We all walked into a bar. A bar, for you young whippersnappers, is where men like me used to go to get drunk. Anyway, let me just say…"

Biden was still talking about his past at the time of publication, and campaign staffers told us not to expect him to stop any time soon.

OCTOBER 8, 2019

Trump Checks Democratic Primary Polls to Figure out Who Foreign Countries Should Investigate for Corruption Next

WASHINGTON, D.C. — His Royal Highness, the Grand Imperial President of America-Land, has not hidden his desire to have foreign help to win next year's election.

Though it's unclear why his Grand Excellency has not seen fit to simply use his "absolute right" to do whatever he wants, and cancel next year's election for the good of the country, and to retain control, King Donald Trump has been laser-focused on asking foreign leaders to dig up dirt on Joe Biden. Mr. Biden, a former Vice President from the Previous Black Administration, is presumed to be corrupt by Emperor Donald, and as such, the Ukrainian president was asked by his Royal Perfectness to investigate Biden and his son Hunter.

The Lord Thy Trump's efforts to get Ukraine and China to help him dig up dirt on Biden gave congressional Democrats — who control a branch of government that is allegedly co-equal to that of He Of The Massive Hands and Normally-Shaped Dong — their window to begin an impeachment inquiry. Buzz on the Hill is that His Majesty the President is strongly considering dissolving Congress permanently, and leaving it to the regional governors to have direct control of their

OCTOBER

territories.

"Fear will keep the local states in line," one aide to King Trump told us. "Fear of this president nuking their capital, grabbing their women by their pussies, and putting up a Trump Tower in their backyard. He wields the power to destroy entire economies and industries, and he's not afraid to use it."

Some have pondered how Emperor Trump knows who to target. Where do his finely tuned instincts for finding corruption come from? Certainly not from his own corruption, he has asserted on several occasions. This morning, His Royal Excellency was spotted circling the White House lawn, waiting for a helicopter ride to McDonald's. He agreed to answer some questions from reporters, provided they were "nice" questions.

One reporter, in particular, asked King Trump where his information on who should be investigated comes from. His Royal Highness deigned that to be a good question. So, he answered it, but not before letting out some perfect rectal gas, though he couldn't blame it on the White House dog anymore since Sarah Huckabee Sanders was back home in Arkansas.

"You know what? I like that question. I like that question a lot. You must not be from one of the FAKE NEWS ANGRY BOB MUELLER CROOKED HILLARY OBAMA'S BIRTH CERTIFICATE outlets," Trump began, "so I will answer it. I will indeed answer your question, my loyal subject. However, let me do some quick, extra thinking, to make sure I give you the best answer I can."

A LITTLE BIT LOUDER AND A WHOLE LOT WORSE

Again, His Royal Kingness farted.

"Okay, that's better," King Trump said. "It's actually not that hard, it turns out, to figure out who needs to be investigated for corruption. All you have to do is go to one of those worldwide website thingies that my son, the smart one, not the two older ones I should've aborted, you understand, showed me the other night. These websites put up the latest polls, to see who's currently ahead to get the Democratic nomination. Can you believe they just put this information out there?"

Another royal fart exited Trump's rectum. He continued to yell.

"So, what I do, is I go and look at this worldwide website every single day. It turns out, whoever is leading in the Democrat polls that day, they're the most corrupt and need to be investigated," His Excellency explained. "It's so crazy how that all works out. I literally just have to look at who is most likely to be the Democratic nominee, and instantly I know that they simply must be investigated for corruption. Right on cue. I check the polls and BAM! I know exactly who is getting away with being a crooked, dirty, lowlife loser Democrat!"

He must have had Brussel sprouts for dinner the previous night because once more the Duke of Dumb farted before continuing.

"This summer it was Sleepy Joe Biden. Now that he's had a heart attack I no longer have to ask China to look into Bernie Sanders," Emperor Trump droned on. "But now, it's looking more and more like Liz Warren did something at some time with or without somebody knowing that was maybe, probably, definitely corrupt. So I hate to say

OCTOBER

it, but...CHINA, RUSSIA, UKRAINE, NORTH KOREA, SATAN, IF YOU ARE LISTENING HELP ME WIN — OOPS — I MEAN, HELP ME MAKE THIS WORLD FREE FROM CORRUPTION! PLEASE INVESTIGATE POKER-HAUNT-IS FOR ME OKAY THANKS BYE NOW!"

His Majesty the High King of America-Land saw that his royal helicopter was ready to receive him. He turned on his heel, ran toward the helicopter, and got on. As it flew away, Trump could be seen giving everyone the finger from the helicopter window. It got out of site before he had a chance to moon the reporters, however.

OCTOBER 17, 2019

Donald Trump Jr. Enrolls at Electoral College to 'Learn to Become an Electrician'

NEW YORK, NEW YORK — The president's third smartest son announced today that he was "going back to school to learn a new trade." Speaking to reporters, Donald Trump Jr. divulged that he had recently tried to enroll at the Electoral College because after doing some soul searching, he figured out he wanted to be an electrician one day.

"And I said to myself, Donny Jr, the world's second smartest man named Donald Trump, you know what you need to do," Trump Jr. said, "You need to go learn a new trade. You've already mastered everything else you've ever done, just like your genius father. But you haven't been learned how to work with electricity yet! So I decided I needed to go to school to learn to work with electricity, in case I ever need to change a lightbulb, or you know, hotwire a getaway boat so I and my crime syndicate family can escape to foreign waters one day, whatever."

Trump Jr announced his matriculation at the Electoral College in front of Trump Tower, with his bionic sex android Kimberly Guilfoyle right next to him. Throughout the press conference, however, Mr. Trump kept referring to it as the "Electrical College." It's unclear at this

OCTOBER

time whether Trump Jr knows the difference, however. He said his father already called to congratulate him, and that he was "really looking forward" to having the president pay for his grades "like back in regular college." The president's son told reporters he isn't sure how strenuous his course load will be the first semester, but that he's confident his brother Eric can handle running the Trump Organization's business interests while he's in class.

"The truth is that it doesn't take a lot to make money when your Daddy is pres-o-dent," Donald Junior divulged, "so all Eric has to do is sit there with that dopey look on his face — which a different dopey look than I always have — and we should be sittin' pretty when I graduate from the Electrical College."

Donald Jr said that while he hopes his father will pay off his professors so he'll get good grades again, he is not counting on his father to pay for his tuition. For that, he'll be relying on a scholarship from an uncle.

"Uncle Vlad seemed really happy when I told him I was going to apply to go to the Electrical College," Donald Jr. announced. "He said he was gonna personally pay for all my books and classes! He said that all I have to do in return is take pictures of a few pieces of paper in Daddy's office, which seems like a kickass deal to me. So I took it. I can't wait until I get to play with electricity!"

The president's oldest son divulged that he's "always been into electricity" from a very early age, and he feels like graduating from the Electoral College will give him a chance to truly pursue his passion and dreams.

"Daddy would always laugh and smile when I put forks and knives in light sockets. He'd encourage me, and tell me that it'd be one less mouth to feed, and how it'd be great because it'd be the dumbest mouth he was responsible for," Trump Jr said. "Now I realize he was encouraging me to go learn a trade so I could pull myself up by my own bootstraps like he did when Grampa Fred gave him all that money to fail at his first six or seven businesses with! What a great Daddy he is!"

OCTOBER 30, 2019

President Says Constitution Signers Were 'Never Trumpers' Who Planned a Coup Against Him

WASHINGTON, D.C. — Just moments ago, President Donald J. Trump accused James Madison, Benjamin Franklin, and the other 37 signatories of the Constitution of the United States, of being "Never Trumpers." The president further insinuated that when the Constitution was signed over 200 years ago, that those putting their name to it were "part of a vicious cabal" that "began an unfair witch hunt and coup" against him.

"They were Never Trumpers, obviously, all of them," Trump yelled at reporters on the lawn of the White House. "The only people who want me impeached are Never Trumpers! And so anyone who literally invented impeachment must be a Never Trumper!"

Trump had been asked by the press pool why he keeps referring to the impeachment efforts against him in the House as a "witch hunt" and a "coup." The impeachment process is written into the actual foundational document that formed the country and is meant to hold presidents accountable to the rule of law. Mr. Trump said he's "not aware of any parts of the Constant-Tuition that give cucks the right to hold presidents accountable."

A LITTLE BIT LOUDER AND A WHOLE LOT WORSE

"Seriously," Trump egged his detractors on, "find me the phrase, 'hold the president accountable' in the Constant-Tuition and I'll believe. Until then? Impeachment, the Democrats, Congress, the Constant-tuition? All fake news!"

President Trump called any efforts to hold him accountable "dangerous for our country, and more importantly my ego."

"Excuse me, but can you imagine what kind of country we'd have if the president were allowed to simply have his power checked and balanced against coequal parts of our government," Trump bellowed. "Talk about utter chaos! That's why it's far more Americanish for us to make the presidency the way it should be when big-brained people that have normal-sized hands and genitals are running it – like a king. I think kings are good. I mean, I know I like king-sized Snickers bars, so what's the big difference anyhow?"

The president insists that because the founders were "so totally obviously biased against [him]," that much of the Constitution should be "thrown out."

"I'll tell you this much. I'm not going to uphold and defend something written by a bunch of Never Trumpers," the president said pointedly. "That's like handing me a piece of paper that says, 'Fuck you, Donny' on it and expecting me to read it every day. Forget that, folks. I'm not gonna do it. And you literally can't make me."

Mr. Trump explained that "only Never Trumpers and dangerous, far-left, Nancy Pelosi Bob Mueller Angry Democrats" believe in impeaching him. Most Americans, Trump said, would "rather die" than

OCTOBER

have his actions investigated. He pointed to his Electoral College victory in 2016 as proof of this fact.

"I won, okay? I won bigly. Maybe technically it was one of the closest contests ever, but in my head, it was a landslide," Trump insisted. "Which means I have the will of the people behind me. Sure, only about half of a third of them, but you get my meaning. I'm here to stay, and no Never Trumper bull crap is taking me out!"

President Trump has ordered Space Force's top scientists to develop "immediately as possible" the technology needed to travel through time, to address the situation.

"Obviously, we have only one solution to this problem," Trump screamed. "We have to go back in time and kill them all. I'm sorry, I know that sounds harsh, but it's either them or me. And I know, I know deep down where I feel my deepest and most sincere feelings, that every good, clean, white, ammo hoarding American patriot agrees with me."

The president was asked if he'd fully thought out this plan to go back in time and kill the signers of the Constitution. What would happen to the country back in our time? What kind of changes would killing Madison and the others make on our timeline? Trump waved those concerns off with a kingly disregard.

"So there's not the United States of America, who cares? Maybe it'll become Trumplandia," Trump suggested. "Maybe it'll get sold to Russia, who knows?"

Trump farted.

A LITTLE BIT LOUDER AND A WHOLE LOT WORSE

"It'll probably get sold to Russia though, right? I mean, let's stop kidding ourselves here," Trump said with a forced laugh. He looked around and motioned to the staff and small gathering of his supporters he's started herding onto the White House driveway before his impromptu pressers begin.

They all started laughing in one, unified, slightly terrifying laugh.

"I am quite hilarious. I really am. I really, truly am," Trump assured himself. "Now, if you'll excuse me, ladies and gentlemen, I have a helicopter ride to my D.C. golf course to take. They said we can even swing by Micky D's on the way back for a Shamrock Shake. I know it's almost November, but the one down the street from here says they'll keep making them for me as long as I stay out of their restaurant dining room, whatever that means. I don't really care, because who gets a Shamrock Shake every day? ME, BABY!"

OCTOBER 31, 2019

Eric and Donald Trump Jr. Are Going to Scare White House Trick-Or-Treaters as 'Pointy-Headed Ghosts'

WASHINGTON, D.C. — This morning the Trump administration announced that First Sons Donald Jr. and Eric Trump will be participating in a new tradition at the White House for Halloween this year. The Trump sons will be waiting on the White House front lawn and as trick-or-treating children approach to get candy, they will jump out and scare the trick-or-treaters. At a press conference this morning, their costumes were also revealed.

"At first we thought about going as big game hunters," Eric said, with pride flowing from his words, "but Diddums said we can't have our big bang bang sticks for s'curity reasons or something, so we decided to be ghosts!"

Donald Trump Jr. smacked his lips down over his overbite and chimed in too.

"Yeah! Big, pointy-headed scary white ghosts," Don Jr. said, also with pride dripping from his voice.

The ghost costumes will be sewn by none other than Attorney General Jeff Sessions, who told the administration he had "plenty of materials" to use. Sessions said his great-grandpappy also made costumes like these ones and taught his son, who taught Session's father, who then passed the "rich tradition" onto the Attorney General.

"Growing up in Alabama as a young white kid in the 40's and 50's," Sessions said, "you saw a lot of these ghost costumes, and boy did I just love the nice men who wore them."

The Trump boys will also be carrying special, Trump-themed Halloween torches, and will set a giant, lowercase T on fire on the White House lawn.

"You know, for Trump and shit," Don Jr. said, drool falling from his overbite.

When asked, the Trump sons said that their sister had been asked to take part, but that she was requested to be by the president's side the entire night, handing out candy.

"That's what the mommies and daddies do on Halloween," Eric said as Don Jr. smiled, laughed, and clapped along.

But what about Tiffany Trump, the boys were asked. Was she invited?

"Who? Who is that? I've never heard of a Tiffany Trump before," Don Jr. said, "that must be what daddy calls FAKE NEWS!"

This story is developing.

NOVEMBER

NOVEMBER 1, 2019

New York City Real Estate Values Have Tripled Since Trump Announced He Left

NEW YORK, NEW YORK — Last night on Twitter, the President of the United States announced that he had moved his permanent residence from Trump Tower in Manhattan to Mar-a-Lago, his resort in South Florida. In a series of tweets, President Donald Trump complained about how New York City — a place he grew up in and that he built several businesses he'd later drive into the ground — had treated him. Mr. Trump claimed to have paid "millions" in taxes to the city, though he's never released his tax returns as is customary for presidents to do, and that claim cannot be verified.

Mr. Trump lost his home state of New York in a shellacking to former Secretary of State Hillary Rodham Clinton in 2016's contest. Since taking office in January 2017, the State of New York has launched multiple investigations into Trump's charities and business dealings within the state. In fact, Mr. Trump and his family can no longer operate a charity in New York because of what the investigations uncovered.

Trump's announcement blames his being "treated very badly by the political leaders" of both Manhattan and the state government office.

A LITTLE BIT LOUDER AND A WHOLE LOT WORSE

Reports from the Big Apple indicate that thousands of New Yorkers have been dancing in the streets since Trump made his announcement. Some have claimed more New Yorkers are celebrating Trump's departure than showed up to watch him be inaugurated, however, those are mostly rough estimates. What is starting to become clear, according to early reports from the real estate sector, though, is that Trump's departure has had a major impact on land values in the city and the state in general.

"New York City real estate was always pretty crazy," the National Association of Realtors and Real Estate Agents Stacy Maxwell told us in a phone interview. "But our initial reports are showing a substantial spike in values just in the last fourteen or fifteen hours. We're talking a rise in values on an order of magnitude like I've never seen before. It's almost like we're talking about a place that had a major rat infestation for decades and then all of a sudden every rat in the city got on Twitter and announced it was leaving."

Maxwell paused and thought about her analogy for a moment.

"Or, like if the sewer treatment plant in a city exploded and got walking, talking diarrhea all over the place," Maxwell further explained, "and for years the diarrhea and his stupid, vapid, worthless diarrhea children stained and stunk up the city. Then, out of nowhere, the diarrhea says they're leaving, and the city can build a new sewage treatment plant. That's the feeling of utter relief we're hearing from home and landowners already."

Overnight, Maxwell says that real estate speculators began driving

NOVEMBER

values up in the entire state and even in neighboring New Jersey. The closer to Trump Tower, where the president called his permanent residence since the early 1980s, the more the values skyrocketed when he announced he was leaving. Maxwell says she's never seen such a huge spike in values in such a short amount of time.

"It's almost like they were waiting for this to happen for a long time, and their wildest dreams finally came true," Maxwell said. "We've heard some people say they didn't expect their property values to go up like this until after he died. This is bigly great news for a lot of people who owned property near or around Trump Tower.

According to Maxwell, Trump leaving New York has made the state "far more attractive" to many different people.

"If you're not someone who thinks Nazis hang out with some very fine people, you're more attracted to New York now," Maxwell said. "If you don't get threatened by the existence of LGBTQ or brown-skinned people, you're super stoked that Trump left Manhattan. There are literally only upsides to this, from the real estate market's point of view."

Perhaps surprisingly, Maxwell says that Trump moving to Florida has not had an impact on property values in the Sunshine state, either up or down.

"It's Florida, know what I mean? You pretty much already know what you get when you move there," Maxwell said. "Though, it is pretty fitting that one of the biggest dicks in the country would move to the state that looks most like a flaccid one. Not sure that impacts home prices at all, of course, but I just kinda wanted to make that joke. You know what, too? I'm glad I did."

NOVEMBER 1, 2019

Trump Wants Purple Heart for Getting Ego Bruised by Impeachment

WASHINGTON, D.C. — In a closed-door deposition this week, Lt. Col. Alexander Vindman gave what some are calling damning testimony regarding the call between President Donald Trump and a newly elected Ukrainian president this summer.

The call, in which Trump attempted several times to extract a promise from his Ukrainian counterpart of a criminal investigation into the son of Joe Biden, Trump's political rival, has become the eye of the impeachment storm threatening to blow away Trump's presidency. Lt. Col. Vindman, a highly decorated war veteran, testified that he was gravely concerned with the call and that he was a personal witness to it.

In recent weeks, Mr. Trump has blasted the impeachment inquiry currently underway in the House. He has insisted no one listening to the call thought there was anything wrong with it. In fact, Trump has said dozens of times publicly that he considers the call "perfect." Apparently, Lt. Col. Vindman strongly disagrees, and actually heard the call firsthand, obliterating two Trump talking points in the process.

While it might have seemed impossible in previous years and during previous administrations, a sitting president has openly attacked

A LITTLE BIT LOUDER AND A WHOLE LOT WORSE

a Purple Heart recipient out of political animus.

It wasn't just Trump who attacked Lt. Col. Vindman. Several of his surrogates and defenders did as well. However, the president seemed particularly offended when a reporter happened to find him sitting in the White House kitchen, eating a peanut butter and spam sandwich all by himself, and asked Trump about attacking a Purple Heart recipient.

"So what? Did he get a Purple Heart? Does that mean if Prince had attacked me I couldn't go after him since he had a Purple Rain," Trump asked, looking around for validation that he'd just zinged the reporter but finding none? "Getting a Purple Heart means you got wounded in combat, right? No, really, I'm asking because I've never been within five yards of combat, so I'm just asking."

When the reporter confirmed that a Purple Heart is conferred upon those who get wounded in combat, Trump took a long, lingering bite of his sandwich. The president rocked to the left and lifted his leg a bit. A small, squeaky fart came out.

"Interesting. Very interesting. I've always found I like soldiers who aren't wounded in combat more, but unto each their own," President Trump explained. "That being said, I guess people are trying to tell me that I shouldn't attack a Purple Heart recipient. That, in fact, Purple Heart recipients are never criticized too harshly? Do you happen to know if that applies to both political parties?"

The reporter nodded her head.

"Ah, good to know. Good to know," Trump muttered as he pulled out a cocktail napkin and a big orange crayon, writing as he spoke out

NOVEMBER

loud. "In honor of his sacrifice, courage, and braveness in the face of an unrelenting Constitutional Coup by Nervous Nancy, Shifty Schiff, and Bob Mueller's 1.2 trillion angry Democrat mob, I hereby order a Purple Heart bestowed upon your 45th favorite president, me."

Trump folded up the napkin, kissed it, and put it in his pocket.

"I know what you're thinking, but I consider this impeachment coup a war," Trump explained. "During this war, I have been bruised pretty badly. On my ego. Anyone of my several hot wives would tell you that my ego is the biggest and most sensitive part, too. Just ask Ivanka! She's seen it all, my daughter IVANKA. If I don't deserve a Purple Heart for my wounded ego, does anyone really deserve one for fighting in a war? Think about it. I know you will."

The president bade the reporter farewell after he pushed the rest of his sandwich as far into his mouth as he could. Trump could be heard humming "Hail to the Chief" as he swallowed the sandwich and ushered the reporter out of the kitchen. Trump turned around to make sure the light was still on in the kitchen because "conserving energy is for idiots who believe Chinese hoaxes."

"Hail the Chef, cuz he just made me breakfast," Trump started singing. "Hail to the chef cuz he used my favorite bread…Oh, hail to the chef cuz he just made me pancakes! He also made me a sausage, ham, bacon, and bacon-wrapped sausage ham!"

NOVEMBER 4, 2019

Hillary Clinton Offers to Represent President Trump in His Impeachment Trial

NEW YORK, NEW YORK — Former Secretary of State, and winner of the 2016 presidential election if presidential elections were run like literally every other election in the country, Hillary Rodham Clinton, has reportedly offered her legal services President Donald J. Trump during any impeachment proceedings against him.

Mr. Trump seems to be virtually assured of wearing the unfortunate title of just "impeached president." Speaker of the House Nancy Pelosi (D-CA) announced today that she had successfully undergone a spinal transfusion and the result of the surgery was that she finally felt confident to officially open impeachment investigations in several House committees into the president. Ms. Pelosi did not mention the Mueller Report or its contents, though many legal scholars have said it contains the virtual roadmap to impeachment, and instead she focused her comments and invective on Trump's call with the Ukrainian president, and a national security whistleblower complaint that the White House has blocked from the public eye.

The administration has indicated it will be releasing a transcript of the call in which it's believed Mr. Trump tried to pressure Ukraine into

NOVEMBER

investigating former Vice President Joe Biden and his son Hunter. On an unrelated note, five thousand boxes of Sharpie markers have been delivered to the White House, attention "Mr. Prez."

Only two other presidents in history have been impeached, and one — Richard Nixon — was forced to resign by the weight of the impeachment proceedings that were underway against him. Most scholars and historians believe Nixon would have been impeached had he not decided to resign in disgrace instead. Support for impeachment has swelled among House Democrats, who won back control of the lower chamber of Congress in last year's historic mid-term election. No other president has suffered such a solid drubbing in the House during a mid-term, and now it seems the Democratic majority is poised to hang impeachment articles around his presidential legacy.

Speaking on a radio show today, Ms. Clinton said she decided to "extend an olive branch to the tubby wannabe dictator" and offer to be his lawyer in any impeachment trial. Clinton said that "anyone who has seen Rudy Giuliani's half-drunk, half-cracked out blabberthons" on television recently would agree that she could do a better job than he could. Clinton did say, however, that Trump would have to get used to a lot less "ass-kissing and nonstop dragging the conversation back to 9/11."

"I called Donald today and I told him that he may want to start planning now," Clinton told a radio station this morning. "Back in November, when his party loses control of Congress, the way he's conducted himself and his administration, to say nothing of Special

A LITTLE BIT LOUDER AND A WHOLE LOT WORSE

Counsel Mueller's investigation's findings and all the indictments, he could find himself being impeached, no doubt about it. Then the dude was brazen enough to try collusion again! I know it's hard to imagine someone growing up in the lap of privilege, who had never been held accountable in his life for his multiple failures and lies and frauds before would pull some shady shit, but here we are. Face to face. A couple of Silver Spoons."

Ms. Clinton said that she feels uniquely qualified to represent Trump in impeachment proceedings, because of her past work as both a lawyer and a First Lady.

"Look, I'm a successful attorney, I worked on the Watergate team, and I was married to a guy who was impeached," Clinton said. "I'm not saying that makes me the only one who should represent the president. I'm just saying I'm very qualified on several fronts."

Clinton said she hoped Mr. Trump remembers they once didn't have all the animosity between them. At one point, the Trump family and the Clintons were not enemies, the former First Lady said. When Trump was donating to both her husband's and her own campaign coffers, there was no bad blood.

"We went to his wedding to Melania," Clinton said. "And we'll be there for his fourth wedding if he wants, as soon as Ivanka says yes. So it would be my honor to be his legal representation in his impeachment proceeding. That's what friends are for, after all."

Despite hearing chants of "Lock her up!" throughout the 2016 presidential election, chants that were lead by Trump and his

NOVEMBER

supporters, Clinton says she would be able to provide Mr. Trump with "top-notch, unbiased legal advice."

"I mean, I'm not sure I could be the kind of lawyer he's used to, because I've never used campaign funds to pay off a porn star and messed it up so badly that I was raided by the FBI or anything," Clinton said. "But I'm sure I can provide Mr. Trump with top-notch, unbiased legal advice."

The best part for Mr. Trump might be that Clinton has said she'd be willing to do the work pro bono.

"Sure, I'd like to get paid. But I don't need the money," Clinton said. "Besides, we all know Donald has a problem paying his own bills, and I don't accept rubles as payment."

The White House has yet to respond to Ms. Clinton's offer.

NOVEMBER 5, 2019

President Requires Dirt on Joe Biden Before Pardoning Any Turkeys

WASHINGTON, D.C. — For many years, a time-honored tradition of American politics has been to have the sitting President of the United States "pardon" a turkey that is supposedly doomed to be Thanksgiving dinner.

Presidents on both sides of the aisle have participated, though, during the George W. Bush administration, the live turkey was replaced with packages of smoked turkey sliced into lunch meat because the president at the time was intimidated by animals with a larger brain than his. When he took office in 2017, President Donald Trump began undoing or reversing several decisions made by his predecessor, Barack Obama (D-Kenya). To say that Trump is unconventional and untethered to tradition.

However, for the last two years, Mr. Trump has in fact pardoned the Thanksgiving turkey. This year, though, he's added a new wrinkle to the ceremony. Moments ago, on the White House lawn, Trump admitted to reporters that he conditioned the Thanksgiving pardon on the ability of the chosen turkey to "investigate the Bidens for any corruption." It's unclear just was a jurisdictional authority the turkey

NOVEMBER

has to investigate, and where, but nevertheless, Trump is insisting that the condemned turkey try to dig up dirt on Joe Biden and his family before any pardons are issued.

"This is about corruption, pure and simple, okay? My call with the gobble-gobble was perfect! Perfect, I tell you," Trump shouted. "The only people who don't think my call was perfect are Never Trumpers! And you know what's not in the Constitution? Never Trumpers! Therefore, technically they're unconstitutional, and that makes them ILLEGAL. Don't ask me! Ask Bill Barr, he's the one that told me the Constitution made me a god with unlimited powers, and why would I not listen to him?"

The identity of the turkey is still being withheld by the administration until it's confirmed if they'll launch an investigation into the Bidens. However, Trump intimated that even if the turkey in question agrees to investigate Biden and his family, there could be new conditions added to the pardon deal. Trump said that Attorney General William Barr was "quite sure of himself" that presidents are allowed to "literally do and say whatever they want as if the law is irrelevant" to them.

"Maybe by the time Thanksgiving rolls around, Biden won't be up in the polls. Maybe POLKA-HON-TISS will be leading then," Trump explained. "That'll prolly make me suspicious of HER corruption. You see, it's all about corruption, okay? Not politics. It just so happens that everyone I think is corrupt is my political rival. Anyway, if I want dirt on POLKA-HON-TISS, and I think that waddle-waving cuck I'm supposed to pardon's got the goods, I'll tell it to give me the stuff on Warren, or it'll be off with their head."

Trump took the opportunity to announce that he had decided to seat himself back at the adults' table, after all, come Thanksgiving Day. Initially, Trump had thought he wanted to sit at the kids' table, but when he discovered that his daughter Ivanka wouldn't be sitting at the kids' table like she used to "back in her way hotter and younger days," Trump said, he decided to sit with the adults again. The president said he still expects guests he dines with at the adult table to dumb down their dinner conversation so he can follow it.

"That's the other thing Bill Barr said is illegal now. You can't say things I don't get or understand," Trump said, shoving his middle finger into CNN's Jim Acosta's face for no obvious reason, while also farting at the same time. "It's all about me, baby! I'm PRES-O-DENT!"

The White House expects an answer from the condemned turkey by the end of the week.

NOVEMBER 24, 2019

Devin Nunes: "It's Time to Impeach the Media"

WASHINGTON, D.C. — Rep. Devin Nunes (R-CA), the ranking member of the House Intelligence Committee, told reporters just before today's impeachment hearing began that he was planning to "put the real enemies of the people in the spotlight" today. Just minutes later, Nunes was giving his opening statement, and it became readily apparent just what he'd meant.

For much of his opening statement, Nunes lambasted the press. He read several headlines from various mainstream media outlets from stories that were published during the Robert Mueller investigation. Time after time, Nunes either inferred, implied, or directly accused the press of spreading conspiracy theories and lies on behalf of the Democratic Party. Though he offered no actual evidence of his theory, beyond his own accusations, Nunes nevertheless made it abundantly clear that he was far more concerned with highlighting media reports that he felt were inaccurate than he was with President Trump's potential wanton abuse of power.

"It's time to impeach the media, frankly, and I'm a little upset at James Madison for starting a deep state coup against our dear president

A LITTLE BIT LOUDER AND A WHOLE LOT WORSE

without giving us the ability to impeach them," Nunes told reporters during a break in the hearing. "We've got a plan for that though. You can change any document with a little White Out and a pen, right?"

The Constitution of the United States of America, in its First Amendment, guarantees that Congress will "make no law respecting an establishment of religion, or prohibiting the free exercise thereof; or abridging the freedom of speech, or of the press, or the right of the people peaceably to assemble, and to petition the Government for a redress of grievances." While many presidential administrations have bristled at the coverage of their administrations' activities, however, few have attacked with such regularity and severity the institutions of the press as Trump. Many have drawn numerous parallels between Trump and former President Richard Nixon, who also railed against the media as pressure on his administration grew during the impeachment investigation against him.

While Nixon was never formally impeached — he resigned after the Supreme Court unanimously ruled that he had to turn over the infamous "Nixon Tapes" — it's unclear at this time if Trump will see articles of impeachment against him passed out of the House Intelligence Committee. Nevertheless, Nunes and his fellow Republicans on the committee and in the House have routinely assailed the process under which Committee Chairman Rep. Adam Schiff (D-CA) has run the proceedings. They have frequently complained that Schiff held closed-door depositions before beginning the current.

Nunes brought up that subject to reporters during the same break.

NOVEMBER

"Why come now we're doing these things in public? Shouldn't something like this be handled behind closed doors, so we don't frighten our Dear President," Nunes asked rhetorically. "Don't get me wrong, he's clearly the healthiest, most robust and manly man this country has ever had as its Commander in Chief, but he's still a man in his seventies, and we all swore an oath to defend his ego, did we not? No? I was the only one who…oh, I see, then."

Reached for comment, President Trump said he was "bigly pleased with Devin's performance" today. Though, the president did mention he had some initial concerns about what he'd hear coming out of Nunes' mouth today when he pondered what might happen during the hearing last night on the toilet during his routine "evening executive time."

"Honestly I was worried that I wouldn't hear good stuff coming out of Devin's pie hole this morning," Trump shouted at reporters on the White House lawn. "Not because I think he'd be disloyal to me, his Constitutional God Emperor King, though. Because I wasn't sure if anyone could understand the words he was saying unless he took my totally normal-sized, shaped, and smelling phallus out first."

If impeached, Mr. Trump would become just the third such man to hold the highest office in America who was also tainted with such a stain on his legacy. The last time a president was impeached was when President Bill Clinton faced impeachment for, largely, lying about a personal sexual relationship with an intern. Congressman Gym Jordan told reporters those lies were "much more different" than the ones Trump is accused of telling.

A LITTLE BIT LOUDER AND A WHOLE LOT WORSE

"You see, we were accusing Clinton of fucking around with someone else and lying about it, and Trump's being accused of lying about trying to fuck this country," Jordan said with exasperation in his voice, "and that's his ABSOLUTE RIGHT! The Constitution says, somewhere, I think, prolly, that he's allowed to do whatever he wants! So why are we here? You'll have to ask Adam Schiff, who apparently thinks the Constitution says he can hold Trump accountable for some reason."

DECEMBER

DECEMBER 1, 2019

Study Shows 100% of Abortions You Don't Get Still None of Your Business

Several red states are in various stages of implementing sweeping abortion bans aimed squarely at eventually toppling the 1973 landmark *Roe vs. Wade* Supreme Court decision that affirmed the right of all women in the country to terminate their pregnancy before the point of medical viability for the fetus, or fetuses. Laws in Alabama, Missouri, Ohio, and Georgia all set the line of legal demarcation back as far as they can, with Alabama's criminalizing abortion at all stages of pregnancy without an exception for rape or incest. All of the laws are likely unconstitutional by the standard of *Roe,* however, it's no secret that socially conservative activists have been waiting for a time when the ideological makeup of the high court is presumed to be strong enough in their favor that they could challenge that precedent with laws such as the new ones being drafted and signed into law.

With so much attention and focus on abortion and abortion rights these days, it's no surprise that a scientific research institute would take up the subject, and a team at the Western University of North Montana did exactly that. The researchers did what they called a "deep dive" on abortion, and focused their study of it on one key element — how many of the abortions performed in this country are none of your fucking business.

As it turns out, WUNM researchers found the answer to that question to be, "Literally all of them." According to Dr. Willamina S. Maychee, the scientist who led the study, a full 100% of the abortions performed in America are none of anyone's business except the woman who chose to have the abortion and her doctor. The results, Dr. Maychee says, are "conclusive as fuck."

"In every abortion procedure we researched, we found they don't impact you, your mother, your priest, your brother, your husband, your congressional representative, your senator, and indeed, even your president, unless you happen to be the one having the abortion, and is therefore by the longstanding definition of the term,'None of your fucking business,'" Dr. Maychee told reporters a press conference announcing the results of the study.

Maychee says that her study is actually just reconfirming the results of studies conducted years ago.

"The thing is, we've known for at least 50 years that abortions are private choices made between a woman and her doctor, but some people in this country get really confused with what's a fact and what's a feeling," Dr. Maychee said. "And of course they're usually the ones screaming, 'Fuck your feelings' at everyone, so that only causes more confusion. I'm glad we could end some of that confusion."

Dr. Maychee says she's "astounded" by the results because so few things she researches ever get proven quite so conclusively.

DECEMBER

"We're talking conclusive results with 0% margin of error. That literally never happens except in the instance of how many abortions are of any concern to you," Dr. Maychee said. "Unless again to reiterate, you're the one electing to have an abortion. Then, that is the only abortion you're allowed to have a say in. You can't force someone to have or not have an abortion if they want. I know that sounds crazy, but we also confirmed that constitutional precedent and the right to privacy are still things in this country for now, so it all checks out."

Reporters asked Dr. Maychee if there are ever any scenarios where an abortion would be someone's business.

"Is the person in question also the pregnant woman having an abortion," Maychee asked rhetorically, "then, no. It's never any of your fucking business. Not now, not 15 years from now, not 50 years ago. Never. Ever. It's none of your fucking business."

WUNM's research also conducted a couple of other studies and Maychee spoke about those results as well.

"We also confirmed that where a transgender person takes a shit is none of your goddamned business," Maychee said, "and it's never, ever, ever your business when two adults marry each other, no matter what genitals each of them possesses. Oh, also, water is wet, the sky is blue, and Laura Ingraham is a literal diarrhea Gollum. But there I go confirming the obvious for you again."

By the time you finish reading this, it still won't be any of your fucking business who gets an abortion.

DECEMBER 2, 2019

Trump Demands House Vote on His Articles of Impeachment Using 'Electoral College Rules'

WASHINGTON, D.C. — President Donald Trump paced angrily around the White House lawn, a couple days ahead of the first public impeachment hearings conducted against him by the House Judiciary Committee. Last month, the House Intelligence Committee conducted several closed-door depositions and a handful of highly-publicized public hearings, all of which Trump and his surrogates have assailed as being unfair to him.

Trump's legal team announced over the weekend, despite protests that the proceedings up to this point were not inclusive of the president enough, that they would not be participating in the hearings this week. They had been explicitly invited by Chairman Jerry Nadler (D-NJ) to do so, however. Nadler's committee intends to start their hearings on Wednesday.

As Trump skulked around the White House lawn, waiting for a helicopter to take him to McDonald's for a breakfast Big Mac before jetting off to Europe for a NATO conference, he lamented the fact that his impeachment seems all but a foregone conclusion at this point. The president admitted that even he doesn't see a way for his administration

DECEMBER

to escape the taint and stigma of being just the third administration in the country's history to be impeached. While his impeachment in the House is nowhere near a promise of removal from office by a Republican-dominated Senate, President Trump said he was going to issue an executive order to the House, demanding that they vote on any articles of impeachment against him using the same math that the Electoral College uses.

"Bill Barr told me that if I want to really stop this impeachment thing in its tracks," Trump explained, "all I have to do is issue an order to the jerks in the House that they have to count votes on the impeachment articles using the Electoral College scale. Billy told me that in his view of presidential powers, I have every right to demand whatever I want from Congress, as long as I wave my scepter hard and long enough. And you can ask Ivanka, very few people wave their scepters as well as I do; I know that for a fact!"

President Trump explained that because he won solely on the merits of the Electoral College's machinations, his impeachment process should be held to the same standard. He argued that if votes cast in Iowa are worth five times more than votes cast in California, then votes cast by Iowan congressional representatives should count fives times as much as votes cast by Californian congresspeople. Trump said all his time spent on the golf course as president inspired this new legal strategy.

"In golf, the lower you score, the better you do. And I've used that philosophy my whole life," Trump said. "That's why I consider the IQ

A LITTLE BIT LOUDER AND A WHOLE LOT WORSE

levels of myself and my family to be genius levels. That's why I talk about my victory in the Electoral College like it was the biggest landslide ever, instead of being the biggest fluke of luck for a loser with a lifetime of utter failure that would have destroyed his career and reputation if his daddy hadn't been super-rich when he was born."

Senator Lindsey Graham (R-Trump's Rectum), told reporters he thinks it's a "fine and dandy idea" to order the House to follow Electoral College rules when voting on articles of impeachment.

"We're still talking about a Republican president, right," Graham confirmed with the press before continuing, "then, yes. Of course, I support this completely and totally."

Congressman and noted goat fucker Devin Nunes (R-Trump's Perineum) lamented that even though he "fully and sycophantically" supports Trump's order, he doesn't think it goes quite far enough. Nunes warned that unless Trump permanently dissolves the House of representatives, they might continue their "rampant, abusive attempts to hold the president accountable." Rep. Nunes said as soon as he gets done suing fictional cows, he plans to help Trump draft the order.

"If you ask me, and I know that only Russians and Trump administration officials ever do ask me, but still, let me keep talking in that stilted, barely literate way that I somehow think makes me sound intellectually astute," Nunes half-mumbled, half-said aloud, "I think King President Trump should go even further. I say he dissolves the Congress, permanently. Fear will keep the local states in line; we don't need three branches of government. That's very wasteful."

DECEMBER

Nunes opined that he worried about Republican senators "spontaneously growing a conscience" once articles of impeachment reached the upper chamber.

"What happens if a few cuck Republican Senators decide they value the country and its institutions more than the GOP," Nunes asked rhetorically, "or even scarier, more than they value the dear president's ego? They could convict him, and then we'd be in the horrible position of an abusive, would-be tyrant being removed from office completely constitutionally! That doesn't sound like America to me, comrades."

DECEMBER 10, 2019

White House: Articles of Impeachment Don't Have Enough Pictures so Trump Can't Understand Them

WASHINGTON, D.C. — The White House released a letter this morning, demanding that the House Democrats revise the articles of impeachment against President Donald J. Trump.

The Trump administration is not demanding any substantive changes to the content of the articles, nor to the charges levied against the president. Rather, the White House and Trump's outside legal counsel are forcefully and formally requesting that the impeachment articles be heavily revised to "include as many pictures and/or full-color drawings as possible." They argue that Trump's reading level is so low that he'll "get bored and not be able to fully understand" the charges against him without a lot of pictures to keep him engaged.

"We hereby demand that the House Democrats immediately revise their Articles of Impeachment to include many, many, many more pictures than they currently contain," the White House letter reads. "This is not only fair to Trump, but also will ensure that he has a good, full grasp on just what is happening. We're afraid that without pictures, it still won't register in the president's brain, or what he refers to his brain but what others might call, 'Jello-o in an empty skull,' that he's

DECEMBER

been impeached until after the vote comes down in the House."

The two articles of impeachment unveiled this morning accuse President Trump of abusing his power and then obstructing congressional efforts to investigate his abuse of power. It's a scenario that is seemingly playing out similarly to the articles of impeachment drafted against President Richard Nixon. Though Nixon resigned in disgrace before a full House vote on them, among the articles drafted against Nixon were those charging him with abusing his power to target political rivals and obstructing Congress.

"It's like deja vu all over again," one presidential historian told us. "You know what they say about history repeating itself? Well, it would appear the Republican Party's base has decided to get on a hamster wheel."

Trump defenders seem to be counting on the GOP majority in the Senate acting as a firewall against his conviction and removal from office. Regardless of that fact, Trump looks to be on a collision course with history yet again, becoming just the third president formally impeached by the House of Representatives. Whether or not the stain of impeachment has any impact on his 2020 presidential campaign remains to be seen.

"By denying President Trump his basic right to interpret the charges against him using pictures and images, Nancy Pelosi and her fellow Democrats are doing a great disservice to this nation, and to the president himself," the White House letter asserts. "If you wouldn't charge a toddler with a crime without some pictures to explain the charges to them, how could you do the same to this president? It's unfair in the extreme, and we hereby demand that the situation be remedied ASAP."

Reportedly, the Democrats are already in talks with an artist to create illustrations to be inserted in a copy of the articles of impeachment they'll deliver to the White House later today.

"We're trying to get connected with President Trump's third smartest son Don Jr, to see if he can take the crayon out of his nose and draw some pictures his daddy can understand," one Democratic staffer told us, "but we know there's a risk there because we'll have to explain to Junior with hand signals what the articles mean. We hope he can translate that into pictures. He's actually, somehow, dumber and more illiterate than his father. Heady times, indeed."

DECEMBER 13, 2019

McConnell Promises to Hold Impeachment Trial in Moscow

WASHINGTON, D.C. — Senate Majority Leader Mitch McConnell said today that "in the interest of fairness and logic" he's going to file a change of venue request and hold the impeachment trial of President Donald J. Trump in Moscow, Russia.

While the two articles of impeachment adopted by the House Judiciary Committee along party lines, they have not been put to a vote before the full House of Representatives. Most expect the Democratically controlled House to pass the articles, with perhaps some more "moderate" Democrats choosing not to vote to impeach, to bolster their chances in next year's elections if they happen to represent Trump districts. Earlier this morning, McConnell told Fox News the Republican-led Senate will coordinate its efforts with the White House, despite each Senator ostensibly being given the constitutional duty to be a juror in the trial.

Later in the day, Senator McConnell was spotted coming back from his lunch break and announced his proposed change of venue.

"I intend to file the necessary paperwork to move any Senate impeachment trial from our nation's capital to Moscow," McConnell explained. "My reasoning for this is quite simple. A president should be impeached in the country he works to serve most. If we had ever been able to impeach that nig – excuse me, URBAN – president we had before Trump, I'd have insisted we hold his trial in Hell, because as everyone knows he literally works for Satan.

While he fully intends to hold the impeachment trial in Moscow, McConnell is unsure about a few other changes that he's currently mulling over.

"We're still debating whether or not to hold the proceedings in English or Russian so that it's easier for our bosses to follow along," McConnell divulged, wiping coal dust off the crotch of his suit trousers. "But in the interest of fairness and logic, frankly it just has to be done in Russia."

Reportedly, the White House is quite supportive of McConnell's decision to move the trial to Russia. In a statement to the press, White House Press Secretary Stephanie Grisham hailed McConnell as a "true comrade of the белый дом." The president, while awaiting a helicopter ride to his D.C. area golf resort for lunch at the clubhouse with is First Lady, agreed to shout at reporters for a few minutes while he paced around the White House lawn, and was asked about McConnell's proposed venue change.

"I gotta make this quick because Ivanka's already waiting for me at the clubhouse, but hell yes I back that! That's, really, if you think about it, a genius move. And if anyone knows what's genius, it's me, the stablest of geniuses," Trump said. "I'm frankly really excited at the idea

DECEMBER

of taking a trip back to Moscow. I haven't been in a while, and there are some very lovely urinary working girls I'd like to pop in on. Plus, I'm wondering if Vlad can do my annual performance while I'm there and kill two birds with one, um, rock or whatever."

McConnell does have a few things he needs to "look into and verify" before he fully commits to moving the impeachment trial to Moscow, he said.

"I want to make sure I can still cash the checks the NRA sends me while I'm over there. I figure it won't be a problem because the NRA gets its rubles from Russia anyway," McConnell announced, "but just to be on the safe side, I've put in a call to Vlad to make sure there are decent check cashing places in town where we Republicans can take care of our business."

CPSIA information can be obtained
at www.ICGtesting.com
Printed in the USA
LVHW090419250120
644798LV00001B/15